D0840161

Black Light

Black Light

Ten Stories and a Novella

by

Ron W. Shaw

CACANADADADA

BLACK LIGHT
Copyright © 1993 Ron Shaw

All rights reserved. The use of any part of this publication reproduced, transmitted in any form or by any means, electronic, mechanical, photocopying, recording, or otherwise stored in a retrieval system, without the prior consent of the publisher, is an infringement of the copyright law.

CACANADADADA PRESS LTD.
3350 West 21st Avenue
Vancouver, B.C., Canada
V6S 1G7

Set in Baskerville 10½ point on 13½
Typesetting: The Typeworks, Vancouver, B.C.
Printing: Hignell Printing, Winnipeg, Manitoba
Cover Design: Cecilia Jang
Cover Art: Alvin Jang

The publisher wishes to thank the Canada Council and the British Columbia Cultural Services Branch for their generous financial assistance.

CANADIAN CATALOGUING IN PUBLICATION DATA

Shaw, Ron, 1951–
   Black light

   ISBN 0-921870-17-5

   1. Africa—Fiction.   I. Title.
PS8587.H39B6 1993   C813'.54   C92-091422-5
PR9199.3.S52B6 1993

To Chuise

Acknowledgements

Some stories have appeared in the following magazines:

"Ango Field" in *Kingfisher Magazine*, Berkeley, California

"Last Hunt" in *Tyro*, Sault Ste. Marie, Ontario

"Puppets" in *Ragmag*, Goodhue, Minnesota

"The Fou" in *White Wall Review*, Toronto, Ontario

"A Day in the Life" in *Crazy Quilt Magazine*, San Diego, California

"Soldier's Trilogy" won Second Prize in the Annual Fiction Contest (1990), sponsored by *Crazy Quilt Magazine*

Contents

"I see a black light"
—Vincent Van Gogh on his death bed

Ango Field

BRAITHWAITE TUNED his ear to the port engine. The motor roared along steadily enough but something in the pitch or the rhythm of that sound told him all was not well.

He scanned the instrument panel, watching for the first telltale flutter of a needle or read-out, but everything sat steady and well within normal operation ranges. Still, something was wrong, or would be very soon. He looked over his shoulder at the suspect motor and turned his senses inward, to pulses the aircraft set up inside his own body. Yes, something was just a little out of sync and the problem was in the port engine. His eyes swept the instruments once more and then turned to the sky.

A storm front, sweeping in from the coast behind him, was moving much faster than the met reports had predicted. This did not surprise him, such weather data as was available was limited in the extreme and highly unreliable. It was often a full day old. The rainy season had begun. Storms born in the Gulf of Guinea raced inland within hours, outpacing weather reports tracking their progress. The front was around him now, nudging and bumping the Twin Otter as both storm and aircraft pushed eastward. Rain, in bulging egg-sized drops, rattled against the plane's aluminum skin. The port engine missed and coughed.

Braithwaite made some rapid adjustments and began to whistle softly through his teeth. The uneven stutter of the engine came as no surprise, he had expected it, he was ready. In a way these first real signs of trouble were satisfying. A justification of the worm of suspicion which had burrowed in him for more than an hour. Confirmation of his instincts as a pilot. The engine was still pulling but it did so with more and more difficulty. It would hold out for another twenty minutes or so, Braithwaite guessed, but little longer.

He studied the piles of black boiling clouds rolling around him and opened the map folder on his lap. The red line of his flight plan slashed across a near solid field of green, like a bright ribbon on Christmas wrapping. At first glance the carpet of rain forest indicated below him appeared unbroken all the way to Bangui, nearly a thousand kilometers away. For a moment he studied his compass heading and air speed indicator, running through calculations in his head to check his position. He moved a finger along the red flight path a few centimeters and tipped the map into the now fading light. A few kilometers further east a river snaked across the field of green. He slid his finger northeast, following the twisted blue line and lifted the map higher to read the tiny print . . . Ango.

It takes a skilled and careful pilot to fly the African interior day after day, building hours in the log book which added to years and then more than a decade. Such a pilot begins with instincts he carried into the world with him, augmenting them with the learned skills of training and experience. Hundreds, and then thousands, of landings and takeoffs from poorly constructed, too short bush strips, long journeys over featureless rain forests, hour upon hour of dodging mountains in tropical storms, hone these skills. These things attained, staying alive comes to depend on planning, being careful, and, on occasion, luck. Braithwaite was a good pilot, he was careful, he was a planner and, so far, he had always been lucky.

The stutter of the port engine steadily worsened. Braithwaite whistled tunelessly through his teeth and tapped a tattoo on the map near the village of Ango. He had known it was there, part of the planning. A short, dirty emergency strip built in the colonial years by French army engineers and probably never used since. According to civil aviation authorities in the capital, it was maintained "to minimum standards" for use as an emergency field. Braithwaite tried not to think too much about what "minimum standards" might mean in the middle of the African forest. He estimated he was over the river now and banked northeast.

He could feel an increasing vibration, a shudder, build in the air frame as the faulty engine choked. He mildly cursed the fuel contractor and decided, when he got back to Yola, he would do worse. For the moment though, he concentrated on his position. Time to see if he could get below the thick, lowering ceiling. The Twin Otter nosed down and slipped into the cloud. Less than a minute later he tugged the nose back as the aircraft broke through into heavy rain a little more than a hundred meters above the jungle canopy. He corrected his heading a little to the east and decreased speed.

The strip and the village flashed beneath his wing tip and the unbroken green carpet rolled below him again. Braithwaite grinned. Good navigation or good luck? Finding the field on his first try was more then he could have hoped for. He pulled the aircraft around in a wide careful turn, keeping one eye on the fluttering port engine instruments and the other on the rain forest below him. He dropped closer to the tree tops and reduced his airspeed as much as he dared in circumstances where he was likely to lose an engine at any moment. Once more the village was beneath him and he had a moment to study the emergency strip. It seemed clear of dead falls, but the grass was long, very long, so he could not be certain. Clear or not, he prepared to put the aircraft down. As he swept out over the forest once more he saw villagers emerging from their huts and looking skyward.

At treetop level he turned the plane along the axis of the strip, lowered the landing gear, extended his flaps, and decreased airspeed as much as he dared. As the trees fell away he dropped the plane to the grass as quickly as possible. The Twin Otter bumped through wing high vegetation along muddy ground. He braked hard, struggling to control the skid and bring the plane to a stop in as short a distance as possible, and before he struck some unseen obstruction. As the aircraft rolled to a standstill the troublesome engine coughed one last time and stalled. Braithwaite eyed the offending motor through a curtain of tropical rain and increased power to the starboard engine. The plane swung around and waddled across the strip to a rotting grass hut at the edge of the trees.

As Braithwaite climbed from the cockpit, wheel chocks in hand, the storm arrived at Ango in force. The wind increased only slightly but rain crashed down in torrents sending huge water drops bouncing like tennis balls off the wings and soaking him to the skin in seconds. The sound of it was overwhelming. Water crashed through the high forest canopy, pushing the tall grass of the landing strip flat beneath its weight. Braithwaite grabbed his flight bag and dashed to the partial shelter offered by the tumble-down hut.

Running head down through the storm he nearly collided with the man hidden in murky light behind a sheet of water cascading from the eve.

"Good afternoon, Monsieur. Your papers, please."

Braithwaite wiped water from his eyes and looked up. The man was wrapped in the ragged remains of what had been a black military raincoat and wore the red beret of the local Gendarmerie. Braithwaite pulled his documents from an inside pocket of his flight jacket and chuckled. The Gendarme gave him a questioning look.

"I'm sorry," Braithwaite grinned. "I was not expecting to meet with official procedures at Ango field . . . not quite so promptly at least."

The policeman smiled as well and looked at the papers. "I am Sergeant Ngwa of the Delegation for National Security. I am the responsible officer in Ango." He handed back the papers and lifted a half salute. "I am, for that matter, the only police officer at Ango." He smiled again. "What brings you to Ango?"

"Watered fuel I should think," Braithwaite explained, pocketing his documents. "For whatever reason, I have engine trouble."

"There is a small drinking establishment, just along this path," the policeman explained, gesturing into the trees. "I was sheltering there from the rain when your aeroplane flew over . . . it is only a few meters. Perhaps we could go there and wait for the storm to pass?"

Braithwaite contemplated his plane for a moment. It was parked a little too close to the tree line perhaps, but there was little wind and it was as secure as he could make it. "Fine," he agreed. The Gendarme ducked under the eve and Braithwaite followed him through the storm and into the trees.

The village bar was a rectangular mud hut roofed with rusting zinc sheets which kept the interior dry with the exception of a few small leaks dripping water onto the earth floor. There was no beer because, the Gendarme explained, a bridge had washed out cutting the village off from all but foot traffic ... or so he had thought until Braithwaite landed his aircraft. They ordered country gin which was served in small narrow-mouthed calabashes.

"Your's is the only airplane to land in my time at Ango," the policeman told him, " ... and I've been here four years now." The police officer who had preceded him had told him a helicopter once landed, by mistake, thinking Ango field was the prefectural town of Ndele two hundred kilometers away. The Gendarme thought that must have been at least ten years earlier.

"But you keep the field clear," Braithwaite said.

The Gendarme smiled. "Each year I receive the same orders from Ndele, to clear the field and burn the grass. Once each year the Commandant from brigade at Ndele comes to Ango, inspects the police post, the village and the air field. It is just part of regular duties, not something I ever imagined had anything to do with a real aeroplane."

"I, for one, am glad you've done your duty," Braithwaite laughed. "When I file my report I will send a copy to your brigade commandant at Ndele with a note commending your work."

The Gendarme nodded his thanks and sipped at his calabash. They sat on a rough bench and stared silently through the low doorway into the wet early dusk. An old hen, with bright pink bald patches where its feathers had fallen out, scratched at the dirt floor near the door, sheltering with them from the storm. The bar counter, constructed of a warped plank laid across two upturned steel drums, held a few empty and dusty bottles and a cheap plastic radio which, through static and the drumming of rain on the metal roof, brought into the streaming jungle afternoon the voice of the faraway city. In silence they listened to a newscast in which the national president was extravagantly and frequently praised, and watched the rain. When the interrupted musical program resumed the Gendarme cleared his throat and spat. "There is another white man in Ango," he said quietly.

Braithwaite looked up at the policeman.

"That surprises you, as well it should," the Sergeant smiled, "but there is another white man here. He has stayed at Ango for six years, longer than I have been here. He is Belgian. A prospector for diamonds. He lives here with his wives. I am sure he will welcome you and provide a bed for the night."

The policeman paused but Braithwaite, sensing there was something more, yet not wanting to show such curiosity as to interest the Sergeant, waited for him to go on.

"The white man is called DeMonk and he is ill. He is, I think, more ill than he knows or will admit. M. DeMonk is no longer a young man, yet he does not take the malaria seriously. His junior wife tells me his piss is dark as coffee. The fever has been on him now for more than three weeks . . . "

"Blackwater?" Braithwaite asked.

"There is no doctor here to say, but I think so and the woman thinks so. Without treatment he will die soon . . . M. DeMonk is old and has lived his life . . . death will catch him soon, fever or no, but I would rather it found him elsewhere. It would be better that a white man did not die under my post . . . "

"I am not a doctor," Braithwaite said.

"No," the policeman agreed, "but you have an aeroplane. You could take him to a hospital or clinic. You could take him away."

Braithwaite pulled out his cigarettes and offered one to the Sergeant. He lit both, put the packet and his lighter away, but made no comment.

The officer looked directly into Braithwaite's eyes. "You could take him away in your aeroplane," he pressed.

"I could," Braithwaite conceded.

"He is your brother, a white man, he should be in a hospital."

It should have been simple and straightforward, but Braithwaite sensed a missing part to the story, something held back, a hidden agenda. Somewhere in the policeman's eyes there were clues to something more. "If he is truly sick and asks my help, I will take him with me."

The policeman crossed and recrossed his legs. His sense of un-ease more apparent. "He will not ask. He denies the fever and re-fuses to leave."

"Perhaps it is pride," Braithwaite ventured. "If I suggest on my own, or said you were concerned for him, maybe . . ."

"No, no," the policeman cautioned, his hand fluttering about like the wings of a trapped bird, "don't mention me! If DeMonk thinks it were my idea he would never go . . . never. Please, you must not suggest I had any part in the idea."

The pleading tone of the Sergeant's voice confirmed Braith-waite's suspicion. There was more to the tale than had been told. As always, when in doubt, and especially when dealing with po-licemen, he remained silent.

"The fever has gone to DeMonk's head," Ngwa explained. He had regained control and was speaking softly once more. "He is losing his mind. He talks nonsense, and sings in his sleep, and beats his junior wife with a stick. Please talk to him, persuade him to give it up for this season. There are no diamonds at Ango, everyone knows that except M. DeMonk. Take him away. Ango is no place for an old and sick white man to pass the rains. Insist that he goes with you. You are his last chance. If he does not go now, he will not be alive to leave when the tracks are dry again. You are a white man, he might listen to you."

The plea, on behalf of an old man, sick and isolated in the rain forest, seemed a reasonable one. Yet the police officer made his appeal in a way which puzzled Braithwaite. Though he could not have said what it was, beyond the fact the Gendarme stared at the floor throughout his tale, something in the story or the manner of its telling left him feeling he had arrived at the theatre well into the second act.

"I'm not going anywhere tonight," Braithwaite reminded the Sergeant. "I'll not be able to take off earlier than tomorrow morn-ing, perhaps noon. I can clear the filters and fuel pump in an hour, but the strip will need time to drain . . . even after it stops raining. For now, take me to M. DeMonk."

"I will show you his hut," the policeman said, standing and pulling on his ragged rain coat, "but it would be better if you in-troduced yourself. I will point out the house."

Braithwaite followed the Gendarme into the rain saying nothing. It was apparent relations between DeMonk and the local policeman were unfriendly and perhaps even hostile. He would rather have avoided both of them and the risk of being caught in a feud of which he wanted no part, but he needed a roof for the night and perhaps the old Belgian truly needed help.

They slopped along a muddy path leading uphill behind the bar, shoulders hunched against the driving rain, heads down. At the crest the Gendarme led him to a smaller track through thick undergrowth of broad-leafed plants and into a clearing. "Chez DeMonk," the Gendarme announced nodding to a low, mud-walled house surrounded by several smaller structures of thatch. "He has a tin roof so you will sleep dry, but he will not permit his wives to set their cooking fires inside so it is infested with bugs . . . do you have any newspapers?"

Braithwaite nodded and reached to open his bag thinking the Sergeant wanted news.

"No, not for me," the policeman said, laying his hand on Braithwaite's arm, "for you, for the bugs. Line your blankets with them, it will discourage most of the insects and let you sleep a little." He turned to go back down the path, then stopped. "Remember what I said. Persuade him to go with you. If he does not, he will die. You will see I am right." Turning once more Sergeant Ngwa disappeared into the dripping bush.

Braithwaite crossed the compound, from the shelter of the trees to the narrow eve of the house, at a dog trot and knocked on the plank door. It opened a crack and a young, black, very attractive female face looked out at him, blank of all expression. He started to speak but the girl turned away and the door swung fully open. It took a moment for his eyes to adjust to the yellow lantern light of the interior. When he could make out the room, the girl had seated herself on a camp cot against a wall to his left. Directly in front of him, across the room on another bed, an aged white man sat wrapped in a blanket, leaning against the wall. His face was the colour of parchment and his eyes a glassy yellow, like the marbles he had played with as a child, Braithwaite thought. Long thin wisps of white hair fell to his shoulders and a chest-long white beard straggled across the front of a fading scarlet shirt. He slouched with one foot propped on a stool in front of him. An old African woman, fat, grey showing in her close cut hair, squatted by the stool probing his foot with a needle.

"Jiggers," the old man shouted above the roar of rain pounding on the roof. "Goddamn house is alive with jiggers! My advice is keep your boots on. Wear them until they rot...day and night....Sleep with your boots on, eat with your boots on, bathe with your boots on, fuck with your boots on...don't ever take them off....I'm Henri DeMonk. What do you call yourself?"

"My name is Braithwaite, I..."

"So, you've come. You've found me at last. I knew you would, in the end, but I didn't make it easy for you...did I? It couldn't have been easy. Still, here you are, though it will do you no good at all. You'll not find them. You'll find nothing...nothing....I'll not show you, and where would you begin to look?" He swung his arms in a wide circle, a gesture which managed to encompass the hut, the village and several thousand square kilometers of jungle all at once. "Impossible. Stupid and hopeless even to try, and I'll tell you nothing."

DeMonk reached out with his unoccupied foot and pushed a cane stool toward Braithwaite. "Come in. Sit. Don't stand there, sit. You must be tired from the journey. How bad is the Touki Bridge? Can it be repaired? Had to leave your jeep on the far bank and hoof it in here eh? Sixty-eight kilometers on foot in the rain! You're not as soft as you look." He studied the woman squatted before him for a moment, flinching a little as she dug into the flesh of his foot. "These are my wives," DeMonk said suddenly. "The old one is called Cressence, she has been with me twelve or fourteen years. The young one there, with ice in her eyes and deceit in her heart, is N'Voit. I brought her into my house last season."

Braithwaite nodded to the women, both of whom ignored him.

DeMonk looked at him, "Talk man, talk!" he chuckled. "You must have something to say. How was the road? Could you drive all the way to the Touki or have you walked even further?"

"I didn't come by road, I flew in," Braithwaite told him.

"Flew! Ah, so you flew in. I wanted to drop a tree across that

strip, but the red-cap Ngwa wouldn't let me. I knew we'd have uninvited guests coming down on it one day. . . . I was sure you
would come by road, like me . . . I had forgotten the airfield. I
didn't hear your plane. You must have come after the rain started.
It makes such an unholy noise you can't hear anything, can't hear
yourself think. . . . It will go on like this for ten or twelve weeks
now . . . it's enough to drive a good man insane."

The old man broke off suddenly and squinted at Braithwaite,
tilting his head a little to one side. "It's not so much the noise," he
resumed, "It's the goddamn rain in general. Once it gets started
you can only sit in a hut and wait it out. You just wait and wait.
Two, three months, some years even more, you just wait, listening
to the roar of falling water. Nothing to do. Nothing! At first I
thought it would be fine. Just a good long holiday, lying around,
resting. I got these women to help, but you're a liar and a fool if
you think you can fuck your way through a whole rainy season.
Can't do it! Even at your age I couldn't do it! Fucking will get you
through the first two or three weeks, but after that it's only good
for passing a day or two a week. Even fucking gets old. You'd
never believe that fucking can get so old so quick until you've got
nothing else to do. Now, of course, I'm too old myself to rely on
fucking to pass much time. This one," he said patting the fat
woman at his feet on the shoulder, "this one has been past it for
years. Still tries now and then, she's a good woman and tries to
please, tries to make me happy, but her heart's not in it like it used
to be . . . so what's the point? I got the young one there because
she's a tiger in the blankets . . . loves it, wants all she can get . . .
but she's a bitch. Since even she can't get me up more than a half
dozen times a week anymore I'm thinking of sending her back to
her father. She's a trouble maker, always fighting the old one here.
Shows no respect. I'd like to chuck her out but the rains have come
and it's a four or five day hike back to her village. You can't force
that on even a bitch like her in the rainy season. Besides, the old
woman is past it, and gone to fat as well. Even what fucking I can
manage will help get me through the season. . . . The bitch is
Takah, you see. All they do is fuck and fight. I'll send her away
when the dry comes again . . . " DeMonk's voice trailed off and

Braithwaite had the impression he was talking to something or someone unseen on the wall just above his head.

"I haven't offered you a drink," DeMonk said, looking again toward his guest. "I'm becoming as savage as the girl. Please forgive me. The beer is gone. No way to get it here since the bridge washed out. Whiskey? Gin? Rum? What's best for the chill?"

"Whiskey," Braithwaite told him.

"Whiskey. Yes indeed. Whiskey is the stuff for the rains. Whiskey for the chill, gin for the fever. Grain juice will get you through. Last year the booze dried up before the weather did. It was hell! No danger this season though. I won't let that happen again... did you see my truck? No, you wouldn't have, you came by air. It's on its side in the trees about twenty klics this side of the bridge. Drove into just a half a hole...it lay down and turned over. Overloaded it I did. I knew it too, but there was no way I could face another rainy season without enough whiskey." He laughed and clapped his hands like a small boy, "Had to recruit every man and boy in six villages to hump my stuff over forty kilometers in head loads. Just like the old days prospecting south of Kisuvu.... We're going to have one hell of a time righting that truck, but I decided to leave it just as it was. No one is likely to make off with it if they have to get its rubber on the ground first.... Of course I've got the distributor here with me just in case anyone is fool enough to try." He laughed again, "Now with the Touki bridge gone it's certainly safe enough...but I got the whiskey in...you said whiskey didn't you?"

Braithwaite nodded.

The old man spoke in patois to the younger woman who sat curled on the cot picking at her own foot with a thorn. She looked surly and then dropped her eyes to her feet and went on digging at the bottom of her big toe. The old man grabbed a stick from beside him on the bed and shouted. The girl spat on the dirt floor but went to a foot locker in the corner and extracted a whiskey bottle. Picking two glasses from the table on her way she delivered the bottle to DeMonk.

"Disobedient bitch!" he sighed. "Nothing to be done about it either. Just one more cross to bear through the rains." He half-filled the water glasses and handed one to Braithwaite. "You don't take water on it?"

Braithwaite shook his head.

"Of course not. Never drink water. Fish fuck in it. . . . You've come late," he said. "If this storm doesn't pass in the next few hours you'll never take off from that swamp of an airstrip. It will be knee deep in water. You'll have to pass the season at Ango." He looked at the girl who had resumed her hunt for jiggers between her toes. "If you have to stay I'll make a gift of her to you." He lifted the stick and waved it around his head, "I'll give you this as well, it's part of the package." He laughed again and spoke to the girl in patois but she ignored him. "Insolent bitch," he grumbled.

DeMonk lifted his glass. "To the rains," he toasted.

"To the rains," Braithwaite acknowledged with little enthusiasm.

"You don't talk much. Government men always have a thousand questions. I've got no answers for you, but where are the questions?"

"I have no questions," Braithwaite told him. "I'm not from the government."

"What are you then?"

"A charter pilot . . . forced down by engine trouble on my way to Ngoko."

"There are diamonds at Ngoko. So you are interested in diamonds?"

"The people I fly for are interested in diamonds."

"Everyone is interested in diamonds," the old man said draining his glass and immediately refilling it.

"I'm not," Braithwaite told him.

"You're a liar, but then everyone is also a liar. What are you interested in? Ask me questions. I've been waiting for someone to find me here all these seasons. I have been waiting for the questions. Get on with it."

Braithwaite smiled and held out his glass for a refill. "Okay, what are you doing here in the middle of the bush?"

"Drinking and fucking my way through another rainy season." The old man laughed long and loud, opening his mouth wide, exposing yellowed teeth and unnaturally red gums.

Braithwaite chuckled. "As you say yourself, the rains are very long."

The old man sighed, his mood changing as rapidly as storm clouds roll across the African sun. "In truth," he said, "they never end. Here we have just two seasons, the rains and December . . . and all Decembers in recent memory have been unseasonably wet. In December I go out for supplies, the rest of the year I wait for the rains to end." He spoke for a moment to the old woman who stood and went out into the storm. "It is time we ate something. The old one is a fine cook, you will eat well this evening . . . the young one is useless in the cooking hut, as she is everywhere excepting bed. Left in her hands, I would starve to death before the season was out . . . if she didn't fuck me to death first."

He turned the amber liquid in his glass, silent for a moment. "Once I read a great deal. Reading is perhaps best of all for surviving the season. The rain forest rots the hut, and rots your clothes, but most of all it rots the brain. The decay is not, at first, as noticeable as the mould on your boots, but when it takes hold it is the fastest of all. All day I have been trying to remember my mother's maiden name, but it is gone. . . . I forgot what she looked like years ago. I had a photograph, back in the Congo, but that was years ago too. The rain and the ants got my books early last season . . . last season was a rough one, no books, no booze and the young one there turning evil. I bought a few more when I went out for supplies . . . such as I could find and could afford . . . but the bearers lost, or stole, the boxes carrying them in from the truck. . . ." He looked up from his whiskey glass, "Do you have anything to read? A newspaper, a paperback?"

Thinking of the Police Sergeant's recommendation for jiggers and bed bugs Braithwaite pulled a two-week old Herald Tribune from his flight bag. "I've also got a couple of novels in the plane you can have, I've read them," he offered.

Behind the glaze of fever and jaundice the old man's eyes lit up. "That is most kind. Excellent. Truly generous of you." He took the newspaper and without looking at it folded it carefully in quarters and slipped it under his mattress.

"I have read such a collection of books in my day. Whatever came to hand. Philosophy, novels, medical texts, engineering books, women's magazines, history, mathematics...whatever I could beg, borrow or steal." He laughed self-consciously, "Last season, with nothing to read, I reviewed them all in my head...or at least as much as I could remember. I decided, if I could have just one book with me here, it should be a novel by Graham Greene...and do you know which one I chose to be my only book? I chose *A Burnt-Out Case*!" He laughed again, "Appropriate in its way, don't you think?"

Braithwaite laughed softly, "Are you like Querry?"

DeMonk leaned forward. "Ah, you've read it then! No, I'm not really so much like Querry, but we suffer the same disease... though I am older and I have suffered the affliction much longer. I am not a literary man. In fact I am poorly educated, but I have had an advantage the scholars and academics and learned critics have not enjoyed. I have had the solitude of the rains in which to think. What is important in a novel, what raises the simple story to the level of art, is the ability not to tell the reader how it was, or simply how it happened, but to communicate how it felt. Greene, when he writes about Africa, is a true artist...his other stories are accomplished and skillfully told...but in Africa, Greene is an artist!" The excitement in the old man's face lightened the darkness of the hut. "Greene is an artist, don't you agree? An artist!"

"Greene is an artist," Braithwaite agreed, raising his glass in salute.

DeMonk stared silently at his whiskey glass for a long moment. "But no. I've very little in common with Querry. It is more the setting of *A Burnt-Out Case*, the river and the heavy bush, which pull me in and wrap their spell about me...warming me a little... holds off the fever chill better than this blanket, it does." He laughed a little, high and unnatural until overcome by a choking cough.

When he could breathe again DeMonk took a swallow from his glass. "But Scobie...if you've read *The Heart of the Matter*...now Scobie and I may have some common ground. Catholics, you know. We are corrupted in our own unique way, we Catholics... or at least we lament our corruption from a special point of view. But Scobie's faith almost saved him. Mine was too feeble. It never stood a chance." DeMonk refilled his glass. "I think it was the rain that finally destroyed Scobie . . . and me. But Scobie always had his faith, his God . . . the one thing Querry and I share is that, while in the beginning we may have had some of Scobie's spiritual strength, in Africa we lost it . . . all of it."

The old man sighed and leaned back against the mud wall. "God, I hope this proves an easier season. Last year the rain was endless. No books, no booze, the old woman past anything but cooking and picking jiggers and the girl turning mean." He sighed again.

The senior wife returned with three pots, steam escaping from around their lids. Her cloth hung wet and heavy from the rain, sticking to the rolls of fat about her waist and buttocks and clinging to her sagging breasts. She put the food on a low table made of boards from a packing crate and dragged it in front of the old man. He placed his glass and whiskey bottle on the table and beckoned to Braithwaite. "Pull your stool over here. At least I eat well." Braithwaite placed his stool across the table from the old man.

"Bush meat, manioc cous cous and some greens," DeMonk announced uncovering the pots. He handed Braithwaite a spoon, "I hope you like your chop spicy? That old woman makes a pepper sauce that would fuel your plane!" He speared a piece of meat and popped it in his mouth chuckling. Braithwaite followed suit, immediately gulping whiskey in an attempt to extinguish the fire on his tongue. DeMonk laughed and took a swallow from his own glass. "Terrible, isn't it!? Its always worst when the fever gets me. She's certain a good fiery pepper sauce will cure fever, make me sweat it out. Who knows, maybe she's right. I've had malaria more times than I could count and I'm still sitting here eating red hot cane rat."

"My God!" Braithwaite gasped.

"Eat the cous cous," the old man recommended. "It banks the fire a little." Refilling their glasses DeMonk asked, "How old are you?"

"Thirty five," Braithwaite told him.

"Been out here long?"

"Africa?"

The old man nodded, his mouth full.

"Ten years, one place or another."

"I went to work for the consortium at Leopoldville when I was twenty-two," DeMonk told him. "That was forty-four years ago."

Braithwaite looked up from his meal shaking his head. "Forty-four years! That must have been a different Africa?"

Speaking through a mouthful of greens the old man laughed. "There have been fewer changes than you might imagine. Granted, I've not spent much time where changes are said to happen...in the cities, on the coast...but such as I've seen are superficial...illusionary. My Africa, Greene's Africa, doesn't change, it absorbs...it swallows, it digests. The driver ants came through Ango a few months back. An old man...well, younger than me, but old just the same...got drunk on country gin at a death celebration and passed out on the path...just behind the bar down there. He woke up when the ants were about half done their business. The screams made my blood run cold. They cleaned him to the bone. Africa is like the ants, it consumes everything sooner or later. The rivers chew bridges and dams to bits, the bush swallows roads, locusts eat the plantations, and what nature fails to ruin fast enough the politicians and soldiers and police hurry along. . . . As for us, malaria boils our blood, dysentery strips our guts, jiggers cripple our feet...shit, if the country gin doesn't blind or poison us outright, we fall down drunk and feed the driver ants."

DeMonk laid his spoon on the table and leaned against the wall, adjusting his blanket. "Hepatitis, dengue fever, syphilis, worms, parasites...hell, I've got warts on my ass no one has a name for!"

For the first time since Braithwaite entered the hut the old man fell silent, leaning his back on the wall and staring quietly into the darkness beyond the crooked rafters. The old woman returned and removed the dishes, refilling their glasses before leaving. The girl sat, silent in the deepening shadows, watching but unmoving.

"The body may survive," DeMonk said at last, "but Africa will not be defeated. If the body does not surrender, the mind must. The assault on the mind is more subtle...much more subtle. It isn't an attack, like malaria or jaundice, it's a siege. A slow, grinding, wearing, relentless siege." He slipped into silence again.

Braithwaite sipped a little whiskey and waited. After a moment he asked, "So how does a man, a European, survive year after year out here? What's the antidote?"

"Sin! That's what it is, sin," DeMonk cackled. "Sin, pure and simple. The bush is hell, the kingdom of Satan, and only the sinner can live here. Those who would come are sinners to begin with, they become sinners, or they die. It's the currency of survival. The price paid. An exchange of the soul for time. Time in which a miracle may happen, the miracle of finding those riches hidden in hell with which we may escape this sodden green Hades and then, in some European tabernacle of our own creation, buy back our humanity."

"Diamonds?" Braithwaite ventured.

The old man grinned. "So, after all, you are interested in diamonds . . . ? Yes, diamonds." His voice dropped to a whisper, "The Touki's tributary creeks are bright with chips . . . everywhere there is trace. Somewhere, west of Ango, there is a pipe . . . a huge rich pipe! Make no mistake, it is there. I know. Hidden in the forest, there is a pipe, rising all the way to the surface. . . . " Suddenly DeMonk's voice was gruff and full again. "Look at her," he said waving an arm toward the girl on the cot, "Look at her. Eyes and heart like ice, but fire between her thighs. My N'Voit here is one of the manifestations of Satan, part of the price I pay to avoid falling prey to driver ants." He laughed again, "Anything good which remained in my soul she is sucking out of me. She is claiming the last installments of my debt in this place. With her, I can't last much longer . . . or without her."

The girl's eyes were locked on those of the old man as they engaged in some deep emotional or spiritual combat Braithwaite could not fathom. Still staring at her, with the fever sweat standing on his brow, the old man went on. "If I sent her back to her father now I might yet cheat the devil . . . but the rains have come and the old one is good only for cooking . . . I've left it too late."

The girl continued to stare at DeMonk, but he turned away, refilled his glass and sat silently contemplating the whiskey label.

Braithwaite studied the old man. The bent fingers on the glass trembled and his frail shoulders shook beneath the blanket as chills swept his body. Even allowing for the lantern light his pallor was frightening, his eyes jaundiced and bloodshot. "The devil hasn't got you just yet M. DeMonk," Braithwaite ventured, "but you are ill. You could come with me tomorrow to the clinic at Ngoko."

The old man's head came up with a snap. "I have a touch of fever, nothing more! It will pass by tomorrow, or the day after. I need no clinic."

"This touch of fever has gone on for weeks now," Braithwaite pressed. "It may be Blackwater."

"Who told you that?" DeMonk demanded angrily. "Do you hold my cock when I piss? What do you know of my fever? It was that thief Ngwa wasn't it? Ngwa has been putting ideas in your head."

Braithwaite said nothing.

"I'll not fly off with you and leave my diamonds for that thief Ngwa! My diamonds! Ngwa just wants diamonds. He wants me out of the way so he can get his hands on my diamonds. He hasn't the courage to kill me . . . and if he had it would not get him what he wants. Every village for fifty kilometers knows what Ngwa is af- ter. Even if I die here of fever everyone will believe he killed me just the same . . . with ju ju . . . to take what is mine. He can't kill me and he can't let me die in Ango. He is trying to use you to get me out of his way. Alive or dead, in Ango I stand between Ngwa and what he covets."

A fever chill gripped him and his words became unintelligible mumbles spoken into his beard and the folds of his blanket. DeMonk slumped lower against the wall and began to slip from the cot. Braithwaite stood, but before he could move toward the old man a hand was laid on his arm, holding him back. The old woman, Cressence, had materialized from the night shadows by the door.

"No humbug yourself, Monsieur," she said in soft halting Pid- gin. "I go lookout for mah man." She laid a bundle of blankets she had been carrying on the table and went to the sick man. Exhibit- ing a physical strength which surprised Braithwaite she lifted

DeMonk's crumpled frame and laid him on the bed. With gentleness which seemed an extension of her strength she pulled the old man's blanket around him and touched his sweating face with her palm. "He be over weak," she said, turning back to Braithwaite. "Attacks come quick quick now . . . and stay stay."

DeMonk continued to mumble through his fever delirium, speaking in a mixture of French, English and Ewondo. The only words Braithwaite could make out were Ngwa, diamonds, N'Voit and Querry. From her own cot, the girl watched silent and motionless and without expression.

"Now who be Querry?" the old woman asked.

"A man in a book. A man who was a . . . ." Braithwaite could not find a translation in Pidgin or French for burnt-out case. "A man in a book," he repeated.

Cressence pulled some rolled mats from beneath her co-wife's cot and laid one on the floor near Braithwaite's stool. Kneeling she spread a blanket. "I hope you rest fine for night, Sir."

She stood and dragged the table away from DeMonk's cot. Unrolling another mat she prepared her own bed beside her husband's. The old man's chill-racked body trembled beneath his blankets and he continued to mutter about diamonds and N'Voit and Ngwa and the rain and Querry.

Braithwaite placed his flight bag on the mat for a pillow, lay down and wrapped the blanket around himself against the dampness of the night. Cressence blew out the lantern. The pounding of the rain on the roof was slackening. It would stop soon. The storm was passing. Braithwaite lay in the darkness listening to the diminishing rain and to DeMonk's fevered monologue. He felt the bite of the first bed bug.

"I fit worry you, Sir?" Cressence spoke in the darkness, "Dis man who live in a book . . . dis man name Querry . . . you begin for explain, but you no finish. Mah man always talk about Querry. Who be dis Mr. Querry?"

Braithwaite stared silently into the night for a moment. He scratched at another insect bite and wondered if driver ants foraged in the rain. "I did not finish because my Pidgin is too poor to translate the title of the book . . . and the title, an expression in En-

glish, tells what this Querry was . . . or what he became." Braithwaite lapsed into silence again. The old woman said nothing but,
though he could not see her in the pitch blackness of the hut, he
could feel her waiting for him to go on. He sighed. "Querry was a
white man, in Africa . . . a white man dying from the inside out."

The old woman said nothing for a moment and in the silence the
rain stopped. It stopped suddenly and completely as though some
heavenly switch had been thrown. "And dis Mr. Querry, he suffer
because of some woman?" she asked.

Unseen in the night Braithwaite smiled. The incongruity of discussing Graham Greene in broken English with an old village
woman deep in the rain forest, both amused and, somehow, inspired him. His heart went out to Cressence and her need to
understand.

"The story never tells us directly," he explained. "But yes, we
are led to believe a woman is at the center of Querry's suffering."

DeMonk's muttering was at last overcome by the regular deep
breathing of sleep. "Mah man go die in small time," the old
woman said. "Die time pass we dis night, but it come again in
small time." She lapsed into silence again and, soon, her own
breathing told him she was asleep.

For Braithwaite, sleep would not come. He lay in the night,
robbed of rest by insect bites. Though both DeMonk and Cressence slept, he knew he was not alone in his wakefulness. The girl,
N'Voit, he could feel, did not sleep. She made not a sound but he
was strangely and constantly aware of her hard silent presence.

Some time later Braithwaite was awakened from a fitful doze by
a scraping at the door. For a moment, he thought it might be a rat
or some other animal from the bush, trying to find a way into the
hut. Then he heard the girl N'Voit move off the bed and quietly
cross the room. The door opened and, the sky having cleared since
the storm ended, moonlight spilled in a pale oblong patch across
the floor. The figure in the doorway was only a silhouette but he
recognized the beret and the tattered raincoat. N'Voit slipped outside and the door closed.

He slept a little, off and on, and was not sure how long it was before he heard her return, but a short time later the first light of

dawn began leaking around the ill-fitting door and window shutters. Once again he slept a little.

When Braithwaite awoke, Cressence was gone and both
DeMonk and the girl were asleep. He went outside and studied as
much of the sky as he could see from the tiny clearing. It would
rain again soon. He went inside for his flight bag and made his
way to the airstrip.

He had just completed the task of clearing the clogged fuel line
when the old woman appeared near the hut at the edge of the field.
Wiping his hands on a rag, he went to where she stood.

"I bring you some chop," she said holding out some manioc
dumplings on a banana leaf.

Braithwaite popped one of the starchy morsels into his mouth
and chewed. "I am ready to go now," he said after a moment.
"Last night I offered to take your husband with me, to the clinic at
Ngoko, but he refused. Perhaps you could persuade him to change
his mind?"

The old woman stood there, holding the banana leaf before him,
and said nothing. Braithwaite took the food from her. "If he does
not come with me he will die."

"He tell you why he no go?" she asked.

"He is delirious with fever," Braithwaite said.

"He tell you why?" she asked again.

"He said that, if he leaves Ango, the Gendarme Ngwa will steal
his diamonds.

"And you no believe?"

"The mining company I work for has surveyed this whole area.
They found nothing. I do not believe there are any diamonds
Madame DeMonk. The fever has turned your husband's hopes
into delusions. You must persuade him to come to Ngoko."

The old woman smiled. "You no understand Ewondo, Sir?"

Braithwaite shook his head. "Only a very few words."

"Now true how your company say. The diamonds they hunt, no
be for this Ango. Your company talk true. But my man find
N'Voit. N'Voit in Ewondo mean shining stone. In your language,
N'Voit be diamond. My man's shining stone now my Mbaniah,
my co-wife, this N'Voit. When he talk of shining stone his mind

talk in Ewondo . . . of N'Voit. He love this N'Voit plenty."

"But N'Voit loathes him!" Braithwaite protested. "For that matter, he detests her!"

The old woman nodded. "Yes, nah true. These shining stones dey shine fine plenty, but dem strong . . . dem cold and dem hard. Mah man tell me, dem shining stone fit cut anything, even iron. My Mbaniah, N'Voit, her name fit well well . . . I be only village woman, but I always think shining stone no be dear. In truth, it be worthless. You no fit chop dem, you no fit use dem make wrapper, dey no fit for cover yourself when rain fall. Dis shining stone dear only for some magic way. Dey talk for something be found only inside peoples. Be so this N'Voit. She no get heart, she cold and fit cut man deep deep. But because she be fine for eye, because she be beautiful, she thief mah man's soul . . . and so other man dey follow too."

"Sergeant Ngwa?" Braithwaite asked.

"My man tell you?"

"In his way. I also slept very little last night."

"Me, I sleep fine. N'Voit go out again for night?"

Braithwaite nodded.

"Nearly every night now she go for meet Ngwa."

"Does your husband know?"

"He know."

"Yet he will not come with me to Ngoko?"

Cressence smiled sadly. "It be because he know he deny go with you for Ngoko." She shook her head. "Diamonds dem thief men's souls. Greed for have all. N'Voit take mah man soul. Men fit buy diamonds, but he no truly own dem. When man go die, fine stone still there. Man fit buy woman, but he no truly own dem . . . unless woman her own self want it. Dis love which my man get for dis shining stone done twist he inside. Over love and over greed, dem come out from same family. He prefer for die than see this thing he no truly get go for other man."

"Yes . . . he talked of that as well."

"All man of dis village know Ngwa done thief from my husband's house. All man know dem meet for night. Time come when

my man go die. All man go say Ngwa and N'Voit poison him, or
say dey use some magic way kill him. Talk start already. Then
N'Voit must go back for her papa's house...she be shamed
shamed. No man go want N'Voit again. When mah husband die
for this place he make N'Voit his own forever."

"You could persuade him to change his mind?"

She shook her head. "No sir. At this late time I make no sadness
with my husband. I no dispute his will."

After a moment Braithwaite looked up at the lowering clouds
and turned back toward his plane. "Come, Mammie, I have something for your husband and for you."

The old woman followed him out of the trees through the wet
grass of the landing strip. She stopped some way off, hesitant or
perhaps even afraid to approach too closely.

Braithwaite rummaged in the cargo space until he found a plastic bag of paperback novels. He carried them to where she stood
waiting. "Last night I promised to leave these for him." He
opened the sack and removed a book. "This one is the story of
Querry," he explained, "it is my gift to you." He took a pen from
his pocket and wrote on the fly leaf, "To Cressence, with thanks
for her kindness and hospitality, and with my lasting admiration."
He signed his name.

The old woman turned the book in her hand and smiled. "But
me, I no read. In all Ango only my man...and Ngwa...know
book."

"You have no need to read it. You already know what it says. It
is a gift, a remembrance."

"My man will want for read it."

"I'm sure he will. But it will be you who offers it to him, and...
in the end...the book is yours to keep. I have written your name
in it."

"Thank you, sir." The old woman hesitated for a moment, looking at the tattered book, then made her way back through the
grass and into the trees.

As the yellow of her wrapper disappeared Braithwaite was sure
he saw something else, a fleeting flash of red, among the banana

leaves and elephant grass. He waited, certain he was watched by hidden eyes. He could feel them, lurking in the dripping tree line, waiting near the tumble down hut, but no one appeared.

Thunder rolled in the east. Braithwaite turned and climbed into the cockpit. On the first turn of the starter the port engine came alive with a throaty roar.

Last Hunt

TOBIAS WAITED BY the window, listening. The idling bull-dozer rumbled deeply, setting up vibrations in the floor planks beneath his bare feet. The huge yellow machine was far enough off that the engine noise was not loud and through it he could hear the mutter of the crowd, punctuated now and then, by an excited shout and the cry of a baby.

The inarticulate wail of the child had an animal quality about it and made him think of the baboons, trapped, on the cliff face.

He made a quick shuffling circuit of the one-room house, putting his eye to a crack or two in each of the other walls, but returned quickly to the window. There was nothing to be seen beside or behind him, just piles of rubble rising higher than the roof of his refuge. Between these mountains of broken concrete, earth, timber, rocks, pipe, roof sheet and mud brick he could, in a few places, catch a longer view. Beyond the mounds of debris piled close to his splitting board walls there was nothing, save wreckage and more wreckage, as far as the eye could see.

Two days before Tsinga had been a sprawling quarter housing thousands. This morning all that remained was the tiny plank house from which Tobias watched. The rest had been reduced to acre after acre of destruction.

Tobias stood, slightly to one side of his window, and watched and listened and waited. He could see and hear very well now. The sun was up and the day clear enough for even old eyes. For those outside he knew the dark interior of the room hid him completely, and the noise of the crowd and the machines masked any noise he made limping about.

Fatigue was catching him. He had slept little for the past two days and nights, expecting at any moment to have the machines push his house down on top of him, or for the soldiers to come smashing through his barricaded door to beat him and carry him away to prison. Dozing off and then awakening with a jerk at each new sound, he waited for the end.

Even when he slept his short moments of rest were troubled and haunted by dreams of the forest and the hunted and by the big old baboon facing death on a mountain cliff.

His bad leg hurt more and more. He turned briefly from the window and dragged a wobbly table into position so he could sit on it and watch. Through two days and two nights he had waited but neither the machines nor the soldiers had come. Yesterday the wrecking and the howl of bulldozers had come so close his house swayed and trembled, but the machines passed and, somehow, the house stood. When they cut the earth away below his window the house shifted and tilted so steeply he was certain the building would collapse, yet its grip on the hillside held.

They were trying to frighten him. He knew that. Why, after shaking his house hour after hour, they had yet to realize he could not be frightened away, why they had sent no soldiers to get him, was a puzzle to Tobias. Why they allowed him to defy them for so long was as big a puzzle as the white men, and Tobias was beginning to wonder if the two mysteries were not connected in some way he could not fathom. He reached for the shotgun leaning against the wall and laid it, closer to hand, on the table beside him.

The white men were something to wonder about. In the old days, when there was trouble, there had always been white men about . . . usually the cause of it but, even when not, they were there interfering in affairs uninvited. That had changed. Since independence white men had been replaced by black men wearing European suits and every bit as capable of causing trouble and unwanted meddling. The white men outside, like Tobias, seemed content to watch and wait.

One, the older man, sometimes spoke with the police or army

officers, but only when they approached him. This, Tobias considered odd behaviour for a white man. In his recollection white men had a great deal to say, most of it incomprehensible, and rushed about sweatily giving loud instructions to everyone.

The younger man carried three cameras around his neck pointing them at the crowd and the machines, but mostly at Tobias' house hanging crookedly on the muddy hill. At first Tobias had shouted Bakossi obscenities when the camera was directed toward him, but it did no good. The white man went right on snapping photos. It was annoying but at least the younger one behaved like a white man. White men were always pointing cameras at people.

It had been white men with cameras who had spoiled the mountain, climbing back and forth from top to bottom for no apparent reason and frightening off the game.

Tobias took the shells from his shirt pockets and lined them up on the table top beside the shotgun. He counted again, though he knew very well there were four.

More than a year before he had won a small amount of money in the instant lottery. He had gone directly from collecting his windfall to the Greek shop and purchased five 12-gauge rounds, saving the balance of the money for gifts and taxi fare to the tiny village on the mountainside where he had grown up. Underlying the joy of his unexpected good fortune, the awareness of advancing age had been heavy upon him that day. The dream of tramping the bush of his home region, one more time, perhaps bringing back a monkey or some other bush meat as he had done so often as a younger man had, with the lottery win in his pocket, seemed for a fleeting afternoon, possible.

He had returned to the Tsinga room and, by the light of a kerosine lamp, worked late into the night cleaning and oiling the old shotgun. He had taken much longer about it than even the slow bent fingers of age required. He prolonged the joy of once again cleaning a gun with plans for a real hunt in mind. The smell of gun oil and the blue barrel glinting in the lamp light stirred memories which drew him, for long minutes at a time, far from the job at hand.

The weight of the years upon his aged stooped shoulders had

been lifted as he recalled childhood hunts with his father and uncles, carrying this very weapon until one of the men, having spotted a fleeting glimpse of game, called him to bring the gun forward.

Also that night, as he always did when the wisps of memory were less difficult to grasp, he saw again the brave old baboon of the ravine.

Perhaps he caught a chill sitting there too late in the night, perhaps there was illness lurking within him and the lack of sleep weakened his aged resistance, but he awoke the following morning with fever. First, coins kept aside to buy presents for village relatives were spent on medicine, then the taxi fare. In time, the fever abated, as it always did, and slowly Tobias recovered much of his strength but all that remained of the planned hunting trip were five shotgun shells.

Tobias, with the habits of a huntsman, kept the shells safe and dry in the tin box beneath his bed. When he dug them out this morning, just after dawn, they were as fresh as the day he had dreamed of hunting the great mountainside one last time.

On three sides of Tobias lay the fallen ruins of Tsinga, but from his window, all the way to the main road, machines had already graded that part of the quarter perfectly smooth and flat. Power shovels had loaded the largest debris on trucks and it had been carried away. What remained was crushed and pushed and smashed flat beneath the clanking steel tracks of bulldozers.

When the machines awoke again this morning, one of the ugly yellow monsters had rumbled directly toward Tobias' house. It was only then he had taken the shotgun from its nails on the wall and dug out the shells. Feeble with age and weakened by fatigue, the hunter had still been able to place the charge precisely where he aimed. Though he sighted well forward and shattered only the lights, a storm of flying glass and metal fragments sent the driver clambering from the machine and scrambling out of range toward the road.

Work stopped. The crowd gathered earlier than usual. Police and soldiers began arriving in trucks and the white men returned. Still the waiting went on. Tobias fingered the shells beside him.

With a sigh ending in a shallow cough he broke open the gun and thumbed a round into the breech. After a moment's hesitation he picked up another shell and slipped it back into the pocket of his tattered shirt and thought of the grizzled old baboon.

A light breeze began to carry smokey fumes from the bulldozer into the house and Tobias coughed again. The city was always smokey and foul. When the hunter caught a scent of smoke in the clear cool air of the high forest he did so with a sense of excitement and joy. The smell of such smoke spoke of another man, another hunter, nearby. It spoke of companionship, it spoke of conversation and perhaps a meal to be shared. In the city, smoke consumed all, it was like the smoke of the brush fire that swept the undergrowth burning and destroying without cause or reason. . . .

"Papa. . .! Papa. . .!"

Tobias' head came up with a start. He had dozed off again. A man wearing a necktie and a suit jacket stood by the bulldozer calling. Tobias lifted the shotgun to his lap.

"Old man. . . . Can you hear me?"

Without moving, Tobias called back, "I hear."

"Come to the window, Papa," the man shouted. "We must talk." The man began moving closer to the house.

"Come no closer!" Tobias warned. "As you know, I have my gun."

The man stopped. "Papa, put down your gun and come out now. The time has come to finish this."

"No."

"It is finished old man."

Tobias said nothing for a moment. It was not finished yet. It would be, no doubt, but not yet. His life was past. He would never again see his village. He would never again hunt the high bush. His wives were dead, his children had abandoned him and moved far away to study in another country. He had no money, the food pot was empty. Around him the houses of his neighbors lay in ruin and the people were gone, but he still lived, his house stood, he had his gun and four shells remained. "No," he shouted to the man outside, "it is not yet finished."

"You will be given a place to live," the man called back.

"I have a place to live," Tobias told him.

"This place is not yours," the man told him. "This land belongs to the government. Your house, like the others, was built here illegally. This has been explained to you before. You know these things."

"No one owns the land," Tobias shouted in a tone he might have used with a small child. "Everyone knows the land belongs to those who need it and who use it. I have built my house here, I am using this land. Why do you wish to break my house?"

"Your government has granted this land to another country so they might build their embassy. Do you understand?"

Tobias thought of the white men. His house was being given to the white men. "When I was a young man we were told we had won our land back from the foreigners . . . now you are giving it to them again? No, I do not understand."

The man looked toward the street and two policemen began walking across the open ground toward the bulldozer. Tobias lifted the shotgun and levelled it into the chest of the man. Then, just before he squeezed the trigger he turned it against the side of the machine. The charge crashed against metal. Spinning away, seeking shelter, the man slipped in the mud and scrambled on hands and knees behind the machine. The crowd screamed. The policemen retreated to the road. Tobias ejected the spent shell and jammed a fresh round into the breach.

Tobias had seldom seen a target escaping one of his shots. He was an excellent marksman and one who never fired until he knew he could not miss. Ammunition was too valuable to be wasted on games. It seemed an offense to spend a round simply frightening a target. Tobias had killed many times, he had killed every sort of game offered by the mountain but killing a man was not possible.

The man, now hidden by the bulk of the bulldozer, was shouting. "Papa, put down the gun and come out before there is serious trouble. Do you hear me . . . ?"

Tobias could not help but chuckle. "Serious trouble? Don't joke with me! Is this not serious trouble?" He lifted the gun again and sent another round crashing into the machine.

The crowd by the roadside screamed and as the shouting died

away the man at the bulldozer called again. "Papa, I do not want
to call the soldiers. The foreigners do not want me to call the soldiers. But if you shoot again we will have no choice, Papa. Do you
know what you are doing? It is against the law for you to have a
gun in the city . . . you must know that. You are shooting at officers
of the government. You are an old man, we know you are not a
criminal, but this is a very serious thing you are doing. Stop now
before it is too late."

Within the darkness of his room Tobias smiled. Too late! He
wondered if the man hiding behind the machine really did not
know that it was already much too late. They would take him to
prison, and they would beat him, and very quickly, locked away
from the sun and the stars and the wind and the rain he would die.
Even Tsinga was too far from the mountainside. He had been dying here for years. When he still had his strength he had worked as
a guardian and that had been tolerable. He could sit in the night
and look at the sky and remember and still feel free. But as the
years tightened their grip, age had locked him away in the quarter
where there was no sky and no wind and, in the closeness of his
tiny house, even recall had become difficult. When at last even an
old man's memories begin slipping away, what remains?

Too late. Tobias smiled again and wordlessly lifted the shotgun,
firing another round into the lifeless machine before him.

This time a long silence followed the blast. Then the man behind the bulldozer was shouting again, but in a language Tobias
did not recognize. By the roadside soldiers began unslinging their
rifles and forming a long line.

As he watched and waited, Tobias' mind began to drift again,
and once more he thought of the baboon. The big old battle-
scarred male he had named Meka. Meka had been distinctive and
stood out from the rest of the troupe even as a youth. There was
something in the eyes and in his restless energy which made Meka
memorable from the first.

Meka's troupe lived in shallow caves and the shelter of fallen
rocks along steep walls of a ravine well up the mountain. A small
stream fell from above and tumbled along the ravine bottom irri-
gating a wild orchard of fruit trees and edible plants. The baboons

had no call to wander far from the comfort of their cliff face. Everything they required was provided by the ravine . . . food, water, shelter and relative safety from predators.

Though the ravine was more than a day's march from Tobias' village he visited it often as he hunted the mountain side, pausing to pick fruit or dig wild roots for his daily meal. It also became his habit to check on Meka as the young male fought his way up the hierarchy of the troupe emerging in the end tattered and scarred, but overlord of his own mountainside kingdom. A position he defended against all comers for more than ten years.

Tobias had been hunting the mountainside for nearly a week when the spirits of the bush led him to the ravine, so he found himself sitting by the stream eating wild mango when the leopard came. Had he seen the powerful cat earlier he might, even with the old smooth bore and his one remaining shell, have saved Meka's life. But the leopard first appeared high up the cliff, slowly stalking its way along a ledge toward the females and infants. Perhaps that was how it was meant to be. One hunter should never interfere in the work of another. The screaming and chatter of terrified baboons had attracted Tobias' attention. The females howled in terror, unwilling to leave their young and follow unencumbered members of the troupe in frightened flight up the cliff face. Within seconds, only Meka stood between the leopard and the nursing females trapped in a terrified cluster at the end of their ledge.

Horrified, Tobias watched as the drama unfolded, the cat inching its way forward, crouching, Meka showing his teeth, screaming threats and throwing such small stones as came to hand. Then Tobias felt his heart fall as, stunned, he watched Meka too turn and scramble to the apparent safety of a higher ledge.

But the old baboon kept pace with the advancing cat, pouring a stream of rocks and sticks and screaming abuse upon it as it crept along the narrowing ledge toward the trapped females. Suddenly Meka stopped. Cocking his head, he studied the leopard below him for a long moment. For those few seconds Tobias imagined Meka had, at last, become too old, had at last been out-matched. Then, with a howl that echoed up and down the ravine and sent the chill of death flashing along Tobias' spine, Meka jumped from his refuge hurling his full 150 pounds upon the leopard's back. In a ball of screeching, clawing fur the two animals rolled from the cliff face and plummeted down, slamming with a sickening thud onto the ravine bottom directly across the stream from where Tobias sat.

Propelled into action, Tobias grabbed his gun and stumbled through the water. The big cat lay still but old Meka, sprawled a short distance away, continued to snarl weakly and try to drag himself toward the leopard, unaware through his final pain that his adversary was already dead.

Tobias watched for a few moments feeling, somehow, both joy and regret. Then he pushed his last remaining shell into the gun and, avoiding Meka's eyes, shot him dead.

Tobias left the leopard where it lay. The hide, presented to the chief, would have brought him the greatest honours a hunter could win, but the kill was Meka's and to steal the trophy of another hunter would have been a great offense to the ancestors and the spirits of the mountain side.

All creatures come to an end. The hunted and the hunter. Rarely was that final moment shared but, remembering Meka, Tobias knew such things were, on occasion, granted by the spirits of the mountain and the bush. Granted perhaps in recognition of the courage and faith of those who honoured the taboos of the mountain. To enter the spirit world through a final struggle, well fought to the end, rather than through the gate of age and illness and exhaustion was the greatest honour the spirits could bestow upon the hunter . . . or the hunted.

Tobias watched the line of soldiers jog toward him. He pulled back the hammer, placed the shotgun close to his ear and tugged the trigger. As his last shell exploded he saw old Meka standing tall on his hind legs by the window, white teeth etched against the red of his gaping mouth, thrown wide in one last defiant roar.

Bend Bend Man

TANKOU WAS A handsome man. A face chiseled and then carefully sanded and smoothed as if from hardest ebony, broad shoulders and powerful arms flanking a muscled chest tapering gracefully to a narrow waist. But at the waist, strength and grace ended in a twisted pelvis and the crooked half-formed legs of a near infant. Mangled by polio, Tankou was a cripple.

Tankou passed his days at the cigarette stand consumed by two ever present passions, the painful dragging march of his savings and the smoulder of a love, stunted like his legs at birth, and soured to acid hate.

Still, to the world around him, he offered laughter. Cheerfully he exchanged gossip, selling cigarettes, mostly one at a time for five francs a stick, or three for ten, and sometimes, late at night, a full pack of Blues for one hundred or even a box of Bensons for five hundred. He sold chewing gum and bon bons, matches, torch batteries, biscuits, aspro and the Tiger Balm known in Pidgin as Small No Be Sick.

On each sale he knew the profit, how much went toward his rent, how much for his daily bowl of egousi soup, and how much into the can buried beneath the dirt floor of his room. Amounts destined for the savings tin were measured in fractions of a franc, but Tankou could do the mathematics in his head as he made change and calculate in tenths and fifths his treacle-like advance upon the magic sum of 267,000 francs.

Mornings were good. At dawn he unlocked his folding wooden

box, opening it to display his wares to the day's first labourers on their way to work. Later, office workers and government employees passed and then women on market errands. While the day was cool the people of Banyo stopped to visit and loiterers hung about the street corner Tankou had made his own. The coins dropped in fives and tens in the pasteboard cash box and Tankou counted down as he had counted every day for more than six years.

Afternoons could pass without a single sale, seldom worth the effort of sitting hour after hour with the ragged umbrella providing thin relief from the sun, but Tankou stayed, calculating the difference between 267,000 francs and the notes and coins beneath his floor . . . and brooding on Rachel.

Evenings were best for business. Tankou's corner commanded the main approaches to the Concorde Snack and Mammie Rose's off-license, and the Roxi Cinema was just up the hill. Excepting the corner between the petrol station and the bush taxi park, Tankou's was perhaps the best located table in town. Sales were brisk from dusk to midnight or later and coins fell steadily into his tray, but at sometime during these hours Tankou would lose count of his creeping approach upon the magic number. Rachel would appear.

Rachel had arrived, from Eboko she said, eleven months before. Tankou knew it was eleven months, plus or minus a few days, because like the savings in his can he ran a constant tabulation. Keeping track of the most important things in his life with numbers had become a habit through long days beside his table.

Rachel had become important to him from the first evening he laid eyes upon her, though at first she had not noticed him. To her, he had not existed until he gave himself away in word and deed, reaching out to touch her as she paid for a cigarette one evening and asking, in the most proper school-room English he could manage, if she would accept a full packet as his gift and, just for a moment, sit and talk with him. Her reply, now nine months and three weeks old, still lashed him each time he saw her swaying along the pavement.

"Sit? I do not sit, I dance! And you, cripple, bend bend man, you cannot dance! When I talk it is with an iced drink in my hand

and cold drinks cost money. Do you have money to buy me
Mazout with ice...street vendor?...No more than you have legs
to dance!" Then she grabbed the cigarette pack he had offered and
strode off laughing.

Her laughter echoed in Tankou's head still, and if it began to
fade even a little, she was there night after night to remind him of
the sound. She never passed without barbed reminders of her contempt.

Malicious fate, manifested as polio, stalked Tankou's childhood,
killing the strength in his legs, bending and twisting them into ugly
and useless appendages to be dragged like prison shackles. Yet
misfortune and evil fate follow their own code of perverted justice
and make crude attempts at fair exchange. In place of physical
strength and grace stolen away, the mean spirits of disease planted
in Tankou's heart a burning determination and fierce pride. "God
sends us no trouble without also giving the strength to bear it," the
catechist had once told him. Tankou laughed at the idea. The
pride in his own ability and determination to, in his own way, be
as strong and independent and successful as the man with legs
would not accept God's interference in the struggle as either ally or
enemy. Tankou blamed no one for his situation, either mortal or
mystic, and he equally loathed the thought of seeking the assistance of man or spirit.

When his mother died Tankou lived for a time at the mission.
None said so in words, but he knew his aunts were not prepared to
welcome a homeless cripple. Finding a willing landlord proved
more difficult than saving money for a deposit on his own room in
town, but after more than a year he succeeded. For months, when
he slept, only a straw mat separated him from the dirt floor, but at
the rate of a few francs per day, Tankou saved money to hire a carpenter to build a proper bed, designed low and sturdy, making it
easy for a crippled man to climb on and off. Every few months
thereafter, as Tankou had money, the carpenter added another
item of furniture...a table, two stools, a shelf, a clothesrack...all
built low for convenient use by a man with no legs.

While living at the mission Tankou was given a three wheeled,
hand peddled, handicap vehicle known as a tricyclette. At first his

pride would not let him accept such a gift and he refused. After much talk and a lecture about "Pride going before a fall," Tankou accepted the tricyclette as a loan. Since it reduced his travel time between the mission (and later his room) and the cigarette stand, he reasoned it would enable him to work longer hours and increase his earnings. From those earnings he would buy his own tricyclette and then return the mission vehicle with thanks. The missionaries praised his spirit and agreed.

"And when I buy my tricyclette," Tankou told them, "it will be one of those from the Lebanese shop near the S.D.O.'s office . . . a tricyclette with a motor."

The missionaries and catechist smiled and reminded him that such a vehicle cost more than 250,000 francs.

"The model I have chosen costs 267,000 francs," Tankou said, "and I will buy it."

The motorized tricyclette became the symbol around which Tankou's life revolved for half a decade. Even as his small savings were invested in furnishing his own room, it was the idea of the tricyclette, and the independence and ultimate self reliance it represented, towards which Tankou calculated the gross and net return on every tiny sale, sitting through rain soaked mornings, hot endless afternoons and long chilly nights beside his cigarette stand.

On the evening Rachel first swayed down the pavement towards him and asked, in that husky voice which tightened Tankou's chest, for a packet of Minties, achievement of the dream was in sight. Then, pushed towards her by forces within him he did not understand, Tankou touched her hand. Her reaction, cringing at his touch, pulling back and cruelly lashing out, stabbed through his most sensitive scars to the molten pride beneath.

Had Rachel withdrawn the knife that first night, the wound, not for the first time, might have closed. But she never completely removed her hand and, at every opportunity, twisted the blade. Rachel's loathing and contempt infected the sores and they festered. Fragile seeds of attraction, the first shoots of love were choked by weeds of hate. With each passing taunt, through each successive insult, the center of Tankou's existence shifted from acquiring a motorized tricyclette to exposing the cripple he had discovered within Rachel. Revenge emerged more powerful than the dream he had nurtured for so many years.

The tone of Rachel's mocking voice made constant whispering echoes in Tankou's brain. Images of the way her eyes narrowed when she spoke to him consumed him by day. Her taunting laughter haunted his sleep. Tormented and restless in the night Tankou, unconsciously at first, began to plot. Through days and nights, spurred on by Rachel's unrelenting abuse, fantasies of revenge began to solidify into a plan. For weeks he refined and adjusted the maneuvers required, and waited for the fleeting moment when he would have Rachel at his table alone.

The time came late one morning when Rachel stopped on her way to market. Tankou knew the most critical moment to all his plans had arrived, yet so close to her, smelling her perfume, he hesitated.

"Give me cigarette, cripple!" she snapped.

Tankou opened a fresh packet of Minties and gave her the cigarette. As she dropped the five-franc coin in his money tin he mustered his resolve and spoke, "Rachel . . . listen here . . . I want sleep you . . ."

For the first time Tankou saw Rachel speechless. She stood silent, her face frozen with disgust, staring in disbelief at him. Before she could protest or begin insulting him again, Tankou pressed on.

"I have money. I can pay you well . . . very well. I can pay you more than any man in Banyo."

When she finally spoke Rachel's voice was hard and brittle. "Your head is more crippled than your legs. I do not sleep bend bend man." She spat the last words as though a curse. But in her eyes greed betrayed her.

"I have money," Tankou repeated. He lifted the lid of the coffee tin and tipped it so she could see the fat roll of notes stuffed inside. "I have money," he said again.

Rachel looked at the green and blue notes. Her hand involuntarily moved toward the tin but Tankou replaced the lid and pushed the can to the back corner of his table.

Her eyes squinted as she assessed Tankou in a new light. "And where does a cigarette boy get so much money? Are you a thief as well as a cripple?"

"The money is mine," Tankou said evenly. "It is mine to spend as I wish."

He watched her shift from one foot to the other and back again. He saw her eyes dart up and then down the street and he knew, already, he had won.

"Now how much do you pay?" Her voice was still sharp and hard, but she spoke in a low tone, eyeing passersby.

"I have 200,000 francs," Tankou said, once again catching the flash of greed as her eyes danced back and forth between him and the coffee tin. Then with a jerky nervous motion she nodded sharply.

"You give me 200,000 francs and I will come to your room tonight and sleep you one time. But you must swear to tell no one." Once again her hand made a small motion toward the can.

Tankou shook his head. "No. I pay you more than any man ever pay. You sleep me one whole night . . . in your room."

Rachel rocked back on her heels as though physically slapped by the suggestion. "Never!" she snapped. "No one must see me with bend bend man. You no come my house!"

"I give you 200,000," Tankou reminded her, keeping his voice as even as he could manage.

The struggle was apparent in Rachel's voice when she spoke. "How can I, Rachel, be seen to sleep bend bend man? How!? No money is big enough . . . "

As her voice trailed off Tankou knew the snare was ready to be sprung. He waited a moment, enjoying her discomfort. "Rachel," he said at last, "I come tonight, late late. I go before morning come. No one will see me tonight."

Once again he saw her eyes drift to the coffee tin and he could almost hear the jaws of the trap snap shut.

" . . . You swear . . . ?" she breathed.

Tankou nodded.

"You swear on the graves of your ancestors?"

"I swear," Tankou agreed. "When I come tonight no one will see."

Glancing one more time at the coffee tin she spun around to go. "Late, cripple," she reminded him. "You come late." The sharp heels of her shoes clicked loudly on the concrete walk as she hurried away.

His face a blank mask, Tankou watched her go until she was lost in the crowd at the market gate.

Tankou stayed by his stand later than usual. Business was good but his mind was in the aqwara quarter and on the coming night. He lost count of the day's sales and profits. They no longer seemed important. Dreams of a motorized tricyclette had become ash, hopes consumed in the hot flames of injury fueling revenge. When the last movie at the Roxi was over he closed his table and began cranking his way to the aqwara quarter, following unlighted, half-made back streets of dirt and laterite.

Uneven paths and steep hills made slow going for a tricyclette, but Tankou was strong, he could manage, and he was in no hurry. He had sworn to arrive late and he would keep his word. Resting for a moment before attempting the final slope to Rachel's house, he pulled the roll of money from his shirt pocket and counted it again. Only 1,750 francs remained in the coffee tin. In his hand he held the savings of nearly five and one half years, but as he tucked the money away he was smiling.

The aqwara quarter was dark and empty when he arrived, as he knew it would be. He parked the tricyclette out of sight in a narrow alley beside the house, swung to the ground and scuttled up the earth steps to Rachel's door. He hardly had time to knock before the door jerked open and she hustled him inside locking it behind him.

"Any person see you?" Rachel whispered hoarsely, tension lacing her voice.

Tankou was certain no one had, but he said, "I don't think so, but I was driving my tricyclette and could not look in every shadow."

Rachel let out a worried sigh. "The wheel of your machine squeaks," she said, "I could hear you coming . . . all the way up the hill."

"Yes it does," Tankou agreed, although he had not noticed.

Rachel made an annoyed clicking sound with her tongue. "Did you bring the money?"

"I brought it."

"Give me."

Tankou shook his head. "In the morning, when I go. I will give you in the morning."

For a moment she seemed ready to argue, but instead she gestured toward the bed. "Come, I sleep you now."

As Tankou began to unbutton his shirt Rachel went to a side table and blew out the storm lantern plunging the room into total darkness. Tankou made no comment but Rachel spoke anyway, "I sleep you bend bend man, I sleep you for money, but you cannot pay enough for me to look at you as well."

Tankou finished undressing in silence, tossed his clothes across the foot of the bed and pulled himself up after them. From where he sat, his twisted legs folded beneath him, Rachel was a formless shadow floating in the darkness before him. The room was close and silent save for the soft rustle of cotton as she undressed. The scent of her perfume filled Tankou's head and then he felt the bed rock as she sat beside him. For a second the warmth of her thigh touched his crooked knee, but then jerked away as though jabbed by an electric shock.

"Have you been with a woman before, cripple?" she baited.

Tankou hesitated but elected to tell the truth. "No," he admitted, "I have never slept a woman."

Rachel made a vulgar noise under her breath and sighed. "You are certain you bring money?" she asked again.

"I bring money," Tankou assured her.

Rachel reached out in the darkness, grabbing Tankou's ears. She rolled backward and pulled him roughly on top of her. "So, bend bend man," she hissed into his face, "sleep me . . . if you know how." She spread her legs and pushed upward against him. "Sleep me cripple . . . take your money's worth."

In a rolling, sweeping moment Tankou's rage, his hate and his drive for revenge were lifted on a wave of passion. Pulling himself with powerful arms, dragging his useless legs between Rachel's knees, he entered her. Yet with her warm softness beneath him,

Tankou, however briefly, abandoned the bitterness which had brought him to Rachel's bed.

Tankou slipped away from her long before dawn threatened. As he dressed, she relit the lantern and carefully counted the 200,000 francs, then counted the roll of notes a second time. "You are a fool, bend bend man. Can small jiga-jig be worth so much?" she taunted, folding and refolding the money. "Why do this? You try buy some one time memory to carry with you?" Her voice still cut and tore but there was true puzzlement in the tone as well.

"I do this for what I take and what I leave, Rachel," Tankou said quietly.

She pulled her cloth higher and shrugged. "You talk crazy, cripple. You talk like a fool because you are a fool."

Swinging himself on his hands Tankou went to the door but could not reach the latch. Rachel laughed and opened it for him. "Come again, cripple. When you have another 200,000 francs . . . come again."

"You'll see me soon," Tankou promised, letting himself down the steps to the street. As the door closed he could hear her laughter rise and fall. Laughter without joy or humour, uneven and unnatural.

Tankou climbed onto his tricyclette and, keeping his bargain, was gone from the aqwara quarter and almost home before the first streaks of dawn washed a cloudy morning sky.

Tankou waited until the rain stopped. Sitting on a stool in his doorway he watched shrinking blood-red rivulets of muddy water snake down the road side. He had intended to start back for the aqwara quarter earlier. It would take nearly an hour to crank his tricyclette all the way across Banyo, but the rain which delayed him would also keep the girls close to their houses, so the late start would make no difference. His revenge must be completed in daylight, but it was barely mid-afternoon and revenge would only be complete if the quarter were active, not if everyone sat beneath their roofs wrapped in a cloth against the rain chill.

The storm was passing now, he could hear the laughter of children who had come out to play in the puddles. Time to go.

Tankou slid from his stool and hoisted himself through the door onto the narrow porch of packed earth. He carefully locked the door before easing over the stoop edge and onto his tricyclette parked tight to the porch. The seat was wet and soaked his tattered shorts, but there was no way he could manage the reach required to wipe away the rain water before plopping onto the trike. He had tried once, stretching precariously from the porch until he toppled over the edge falling in a bruised heap in the muddy street. The fall had stunned him but his physical injuries were minor compared to the painful laughter of the children he had endured as they ran to right him and lift him from the muck and onto the tricyclette. The wet seat was uncomfortable, but far less so than the alternative.

It had rained more than he had realized. As he lowered his weight onto the tricyclette he could feel it sink into the muddy path. Tankou pulled on the crank handles moving the machine forward a few inches, but no more. He tried backing up and twisted the front wheel to and fro, but could not move. Before he could even look around for help he heard the Bakossi woman who lived across the street shout, sending a half dozen of her older children skidding through the mud to his aid.

As the youngsters noisily shoved him up the sloping track toward the paved street he waved his appreciation and thought, just for a moment, of the independence a motor-driven tricyclette, with fat tires that did not cut into the mud, would have brought him. At the tarred road the children pushed at a run until they were out of breath, then shoved him on his way with a final shout. Almost absently he called back thanks. Already his mind had left the now empty dream of a motorized tricyclette and was again brooding on Rachel.

Crossing the town in rain Tankou followed only paved roads. These did not trace the shortest route to the aqwara quarter, but today more direct earth tracks were impassable for his hand powered locomotion. As it was, to reach Rachel's house Tankou had to ask assistance from another group of children to push him off the paved street, through fifty meters of greasy laterite, and up the hill. As always he hated begging assistance, but this time he minded a little less. Arriving at Rachel's door amid a crowd of youngsters shouting loud encouragement to each other, attracted the kind of general attention which fitted well with his plans.

He spent a little longer making jokes with his helpers and, as they began to leave, called out his thanks more loudly than usual. The hubbub had the desired effect. The women of the quarter, still idling about their rooms in the chill of a wet afternoon, were drawn to their doorways and porches and windows by the commotion of his arrival.

"Tankou! Have those children kidnapped you?" a tall light-skinned girl laughed from an open door.

Tankou grinned and waved. "No Beatrice. They have pushed me to my destination."

"You've come to see Rachel?" Beatrice was still laughing but the note of surprise was clear in her voice.

"I have. I have come to see Rachel," Tankou called back a little more loudly than was really necessary.

"Rachel! Rachel-o" another girl called from a house across the street.

"Rachel! I say, Rachel, you have a visitor," a third shouted.

All doors and windows in the immediate area were open now and filled with curious faces. Others drifted toward the shouting from further down the street, clustering on porches and doorsteps near Tankou, whispering and giggling amongst themselves. Because of the mud, none stood in the street, and Tankou sat alone, near the steps to Rachel's room.

"Rachel!" someone shouted again. "Tankou has come to see you. Do we bolt our doors in this quarter when a man comes to call?" Amid mounting hilarity there were more calls for Rachel to come out. "Come Rachel, come welcome your guest."

Slowly the door opened and she stood, staring stone-faced into the street. From nowhere it seemed the feeling of haunting tenderness he had once felt for her welled up in Tankou's chest. Even wearing her kabba and with her hair tied in a faded cloth, even with the cruelty and anger flashing in her eyes, she was the most beautiful, desirable woman he had ever seen. He had held this woman in his arms, naked and smooth and warm. He had shared her bed. The only woman he had ever held, the only time he had

ever felt the warmth of a woman's bed. He tried to speak, but
could not. It was as though, by just standing there, she cast a spell
over him completing the paralysis begun by polio. His mouth was
dry and his throat choked off by hot unseen fingers.

He tried to tell her why he had come. He tried to finish what he
had so carefully planned and so cleverly begun at such high cost.
His mouth opened, but the words, rehearsed so often in his mind,
stayed lodged there and would not pass his tongue.

Rachel's eyes burned him. An inarticulate hum of whispers rose
from the expanding crowd around them. Tankou struggled to finish what he had started but his will vanished. He moved to go,
jerking the crank of his tricyclette and turning down hill.

"Go, bend bend man..." The hiss behind him came with the
sting of a knotted whip on an unhealed wound. "Go back to counting your small money and practising your dance steps. Go back to
your impossible dreams. Don't ever again block my stoop with
your peddle cart... this curb is reserved for motor cars. Cars with
four wheels..."

Tankou stopped and turned back. This time he hesitated only a
moment before he spoke, "I will be gone soon Rachel. I will be
gone when I have recovered what I left behind last night."

Watching her he saw the hate in her eyes give way to fear.
"... What are you talking about, cripple?"

"I have forgotten to take my identity card from your room. Go
find it... bring it to me... and I will go."

The buzz of the crowd rose to a roar of astonishment. The fear
in her eyes, he could see, was turning to panic.

"Don't joke with me, bend bend man," she hissed. "How could
your card be in my room? When could you have left anything in
my room?" Her eyes squinted with menace.

"Did you not sleep me last night, Rachel? Did I not pay you
200,000 francs to sleep me last night? Was I not..."

Tankou's voice was drowned in a roar of shouts from the street.
Rachel stamped her foot.

"Me?! Me?! Rachel?! Me sleep a cripple boy who sells bon bons
and matches..." her voice trailed off, breathless. The quarter
roared amazement at the scene they witnessed. Voices shouted.

"Tankou? You sleep this Rachel? Now true, Tankou?"

"You deny, Rachel?"

"This boy pay 200,000 francs, Rachel?"

"Tankou man! Can even Rachel give value for 200,000?"

"Rachel, you over dear!"

"I sleep you for only l00,000 Tankou.... Come see me next time."

Tankou sat in silence waiting. Rachel's eyes, hunted, darted and swept over the howling crowd.

"I deny!" she screamed above the roar. "I deny! I deny! I never sleep this bend bend man!"

"Tankou say he leave his card," someone called. "Let him look."

"No! Never!" she howled, fury causing her voice to break and squeak. "This boy never came in my room and he will not come in now! He has his card in his pocket and will pretend to find it. I deny!"

"Then let someone else look . . . while Tankou waits here."

"No, this is my room. No one comes in my room!"

"You fear, Rachel. Maybe Tankou tells the truth." The crowd roared in pleasure.

"Is true you sleep this aqwara, Tankou?"

Tankou paused for effect. "I sleep this woman last night and I forgot my identity card. I have come to collect it."

As the crowd screamed its laughter louder still, a whistle pierced the uproar. Two policemen, attracted by the noisy crowd, made their way up the slippery street toward Tankou. The crowd applauded the new development.

"What passes here?" one of the officers demanded. "Who is disturbing the peace."

"Tankou says this Rachel woman thief his identity card," a Metis girl shouted from her window.

The policeman looked at Tankou. "True?"

"She no thief my card. I forgot it last night in her room. I . . . "

"You lie!" Rachel screamed hysterically. "You lie! You lie! You lie!"

"Shut up!" The second police officer snapped at Rachel. Turning to Tankou he asked, puzzled, "Now how you leave your card in this aqwara's room?"

"I sleep me this woman. I forget my card. I want it back."

The policeman looked annoyed. "You sleep this woman...? Now talk true."

Tankou looked at Rachel and hesitated. She stared back, consumed by terror and hate. "Enough, cripple. This is enough..." Her voice cut like a razor in soft flesh.

Tankou turned back to the policeman. "Me I sleep this woman. I pay this aqwara 200,000 francs and she sleep me. I left my card in her room. I have come for my card."

The policeman slapped Tankou's face with the flat of his hand, snapping his head with a crack against the hand crank of the tricyclette. A trickle of blood dripped from the corner of Tankou's mouth. The crowd gasped and fell silent.

"Now talk true!" the police officer growled. "No one pays aqwara 200,000 francs... and where does a crippled cigarette boy find 200,000 francs?"

Tankou raised his face again to the policeman. "Beat me if you will, but I talk true."

The police officer strode through the mud toward Rachel. At the door he turned back to Tankou. "When we find no card, Tankou, we'll lock you..." Tankou sat in silence watching the policemen and Rachel. The policeman sighed. "Very well... where should we look?" The crowd regained its sense of theater and cheered.

"Under the mattress. On the side where the bed touches the wall," Tankou said softly.

"No!" Rachel screamed in terror, clawing at the policeman. He pushed her roughly aside and disappeared through the door. Rachel leaned against the wall for a moment and then, face buried in her hands, slid down until she lay curled in the mud of the porch floor.

The policeman was out of sight for less than a minute. As he reappeared the crowd fell silent. Stepping down from the porch he handed Tankou his identity card. Waving a dismissive hand toward Rachel crumpled in the mud he asked, "How could this be worth so much?"

Tankou turned his tricyclette down hill and lurched away in silence.

Soldier's Trilogy

YONKUP:

They want me for a soldier.

Big men from Mamfa have come and their loudspeaker car passed through the quarters summoning everyone to what is called a Patriots' Rally. Mamfa is our subdivisional town and everyone who comes from Mamfa wears a uniform. Policemen, health inspectors, tax collectors, all come from Mamfa. The SDO wears a black suit with a white shirt and neck tie, but it is a uniform. He has no badges or brass buttons or leather belt, but it is the uniform of the really big men. The men and the uniform before which even soldiers and tax collectors stand with lowered eyes. This afternoon the soldiers came.

They want me for a soldier and I am afraid. Since a week now the radio has talked of the north tearing Banga in two. On market day the police inspector came with four constables from Mamfa and took Mallam Garba away. Mallam Garba was putting the first pieces of soja on his brazier when they seized him and beat him there in front of the Banga-Bey off-license. Everyone rushed to see. The constables spit on Mallam Garba and chained his hands and feet. The Inspector shouted that Mallam Garba was a rebel and a spy, that all Banga patriots must guard against traitors who lurk in their villages. I am seventeen and Mallam Garba has been an old man selling spicy soja near the Banga-Bey all my life. He is blind in one eye and has often turned that eye to his brazier when I came hungry from school with no coins.

In the market they say all my age mates are to become soldiers, that Banga needs many men. The market women and men in the beer halls talk and talk. It is said President Kewani is dead and a northerner lives in government house at Yala. It seems now I have never been told the childhood village of President Kewani. Like Mallam Garba at the Banga-Bey, Massa Kewani has always been there in Yala. Somewhere a clan must mourn and the women go bare breasted, but in Banso, Yala and Massa Kewani have always been far away. Today the soldiers and their loudspeaker have brought them nearer.

In only twenty-seven days I was to take up higher studies in Mamfa. I have won my school-leaving certificate and I have passed the Holy Cross Technical College competitive examination. My mother has paid my first-term fees and, with money earned selling yams from my farm, I have bought my tin box and towels and sheets and canvas shoes. Why must I go for a soldier?

Injang has said she will marry me. Mama has spoken to her uncle and they are agreed. At Holy Cross I will learn about radios and cassette players and other electrical things that go wrong. On completion of successful studies Holy Cross gives its boys a box of tools and a small loan with which to begin. In two years I would have a shop and Injang for my wife. How can I go for a soldier?

AMBE:

I am to be a soldier-man. Like my forefathers I am to be a warrior and win honour and respect defending the Bansa.

The big men have come from Mamfa to offer us our place in the struggle. What the radio has been saying is true. The big men have a loudspeaker car and it has explained to the whole village that the northerners are turning again to their old ways. They wish to rule Banga as slave masters once more. They have already taken part of our country away.

As soon as the big men arrived the secretary of the party youth wing sent for me. I was presented to the Mamfa big men and they all shook my hand, even the army Major. I was praised for my letter about Mallam Garba and I was allowed to be the first Bansa boy to put his name and thumb print in the Major's book. The big men told the party secretary I had honoured myself as a Banga patriot twice in one week.

INJANG: .

I understand nothing. Only two weeks ago everything was put in order. Yonkup succeeded in his certificate examinations and won a seat at Mamfa Holy Cross. His Mama came to my Uncle and all was agreed that in only two years Yonkup would take me as his wife. Today the uniforms have come bringing war and all is disorder. Yonkup is to go for a soldier.

I am afraid. Perhaps Yonkup will be lost in the fighting or the war will go on and on and I will be left without a husband until I will no longer be able to give him children. I am also afraid that if the Bansa boys do not go it will be as the loudspeaker tells. The northerners will come into the high country and we will be raped and carried down to the hot lands as slaves.

I have started to clear a new farm for my husband. We have found a piece of land halfway between the river and the farm which Chief Archerimbe says we may use to build our house. Yonkup's cousin has offered one room in his house, across the street from the Banga-Bey, as a shop when Yonkup has learned to mend electrical things.

They will take him for a soldier and my heart cries out against it.

YONKUP:

Ambe came to my house wearing his party sash and carrying a Banga flag. The party secretary is offering real cloth flags to those boys who present themselves to the Major and sign their names in his book. Tomorrow Ambe will leave Bansa and exchange his youth wing sash of red and yellow and blue for another uniform. He was very excited, singing bits of President Kewani praise songs and laughing. Perhaps he has not heard Massa Kewani is no longer at Yala. Ambe says he is to be paid forty Kewans each month for soldiering, with free chop and two uniforms and new boots. The Major also said, Ambe told me, that when he reaches Mera the northern girls, so tall and light, will welcome their liberators as our warrior ancestors have always been honoured in victory.

Ambe is big and awkward. Injang has told me her sisters and age mates say he looks too much like his father's donkey. They think him a bit foolish. Ambe failed all four papers and was not awarded his school leaving certificate. The gari boys in the market say his father beat him. Ambe is happy to go for a soldier and angry that I do not wish to join him.

AMBE:

The big men do not care that I have no school-leaving certificate. Patriotism and a brave heart make a soldier man, not pieces of paper presented by skinny men with eye glasses and hands soft like a woman. No more will father beat me. I am to go for a soldier.

Soon I will have a uniform, one finer even than the tax collector who stays in my father's house when he comes from Mamfa. These silly village girls will see a Bansa warrior. Even that clever child Injang will guard her tongue and think again about the kind of man chosen for her husband. Unlike school boys, soldiers earn salary with which to buy presents and tomorrow I go for a soldier.

Yonkup does not want to be a soldier. I think he is afraid and jealous that, as a soldier, his certificate will earn him no more salary than me. That as a soldier honour is earned by the strong heart, not the clever head. Perhaps that Injang girl has also put a spell on him which saps his courage and leads him to prefer the company of women and white priests in skirts to the warrior camp of his age mates.

Banga needs all its warriors. Yonkup must join me as a soldier.

YONKUP:

Ambe pressed me to go with him to the Patriots' Rally at the party office. I did not wish to go, because I have no sash and did not want to pay money from my school fee savings to buy one. Youth wing militants selling memberships are very difficult to avoid. I also feared the Major with his book of names. Mother said I must go, lest party militants note my absence and make trouble for our family. Injang was going. She sings in her school choir and was summoned to help with the program. So I went.

We walked together from her uncle's house and she held my hand until we came to where the pressure lamps lit the street and the gathering people. Children had brought baskets to collect the termites which fly at this season. Drawn by the many lights, insects were crashing and dying against the lamps. The street was a carpet of squirming, injured termites waiting to be scooped up by laughing children. I found a place on the step of the rice shop, across the street, far back in the crowd. I could see Ambe standing at attention in the rank of boys who had already signed the Major's book.

It must be true that President Kewani is no longer at Yala. Injang and her sisters sang the Banga national song and some party songs, they sang Onward Christian Soldiers and another church hymn, but there were no Massa Kewani praise songs. Everyone looked uneasy when the music ended and there had been no songs for Massa Kewani.

There was much palaver and the people shouted and clapped. The party secretary made a speech and the youth wing chairman made a longer speech. Old Chief Archerimbe talked in Bansa but he could not be heard above the cries of the children catching termites. His voice has not been heard for many years and he looked very old and very tired as two soldiers helped him stand on the beer crate and helped him down again.

The Major from Mamfa spoke last. His words and his manner brought fear. As he talked terror came down from the north and along the crowded street and into the hearts of the Bansa people. When the Major spoke no one shouted or clapped. Even the children were hushed. The people listened silent and still. Though the season is now warm it seemed the damp chill of December slipped off the mountains and flowed around us.

The Major said nothing of Massa Kewani, but made his appeal to the people of Bansa in the name of the party and in the name of a General called Jata. His words called upon every strong man to join General Jata in liberating and reuniting Banga. He warned of rebels marching from the north, into the high homeland of the Bansa, burning crops and villages, violating wives and daughters, killing men and children alike, and taking slaves as was done in the days of our ancestors.

The Major said the Bansa people must sacrifice much to save life and honour in their villages. Then he announced a long list of decrees made by General Jata. There will be new taxes in money and produce so the sons of Bansa joining the army may be fed and armed. The people must also apply to the party for ration cards to buy cooking oil, kerosine, sugar and many other things. Only those families with sons and fathers in the struggle will be issued cards. There are to be no public gatherings. Death celebrations and marriages must be postponed until Banga is whole again. Schools and colleges are closed until all of Banga is liberated.

I am to go for a soldier and I am afraid.

Injang:

I was called to sing with my classmates at the Patriots' Rally, but there was no music in me today. Yonkup walked with me to the party office but stood across the street as though he were trying to hide from it all in the doorway of the rice shop.

When he heard the decrees he seemed turned to wood. He stood unmoving, even his eyes did not blink as he stared at the Mamfa soldier reading the words of General Jata. I had to cover my mouth lest I cry out. It was when I heard the decrees that I knew my man was truly being taken for a soldier.

Everything in Bansa and all of Banga has been turned upside down. The party secretary told us to sing no Massa Kewani praise songs while that gari boy Ambe stood beside the big men and was treated with honour and respect.

Yonkup and I started home from the rally but we stopped by the river. I have shamed my family and now I shame myself more with tears. But I could not and I cannot help myself. My heart is breaking.

My man is to go for a soldier.

AMBE:

Perhaps Mallam Garba is not the only rebel in Bansa. Our people were shamed this night. Even within the secret societies there are those without the stomach to defend our homeland against the slaving northerners. When the ju-ju were called out at the Patriots' Rally they came with the spider mask. The leopard of strength and power remained hidden. I was shamed. It is only good fortune that the Major does not recognize the Bansa masks. Had General Jata learned of our cowardice he might have left Bansa lands open to the slavers.

But General Jata is wise. His decrees have assured that even the cowardly will join in reuniting Banga and defeating the northern rebels once and for all.

At the rally Yonkup stood far across the street but I saw him. His mother can afford the Holy Cross school fees, even though his father is dead, because he is her only son. But General Jata has made provision for the Yonkups of Bansa.

I have been searching for Yonkup since the rally but he has not gone to his house and I cannot find him in the town. Perhaps he has run off to hide in the bush as they say some Mamfa boys have done. We will find him. Yonkup will go for a soldier.

YONKUP:

When the Major climbed down from the beer crate Chief Acherimbe called out the ju-ju. They came led by the spider mask of wisdom, yet the dance spoke of trouble and confusion even among the ancestors. It was a dance of uncertainty. The Major is not a Bansa man and, unaware of the meaning of the masks, was not displeased.

Injang held my hand very tightly as we started home. She led me to the shelter of some eucalyptus trees beside the stream, near the place where women wash their bitter leaf. We have broken our country fashion. We have lain together as man and woman before the bride price has been paid. It is a time of confusion, a night of fear and loneliness. Even the ancestors are troubled.

From where we lie I can see the moon floating above the trees and I wonder if it will look the same for a soldier far from his village. I wonder if I will ever again see it reflecting on this Bansa stream. I wonder how long it may be until I can return with the bride price and seek forgiveness from the ancestors for what Injang and I have done.

Injang is silent, but her face is wet.

I am to go for a soldier and I am afraid.

The Fou

HE PASSES FAITHFULLY. Not at the same time each day, nor even every day, but I know he will come.

He has come for many months now, for more than a year. Even longer than that perhaps. This mad man, the Fou as he's called, always comes. Though I sit with my back to the window, so the light falls most effectively across my desk, suddenly I feel him there.

I wonder how often he passed through this street, behind me and two floors down, before I took notice. It is likely he has done so a thousand or more times. But I don't believe it. That dumpster, or the steel bin which passes for a dumpster here, was there when I first occupied this office. Even then it was planted deep, growing, from its mound of spilled refuse. The garbage bin must have been in its place, blocking the cracked sidewalk, since God created the earth.

. . . Or at least since man created garbage and the need for dumpsters.

. . . It is for the bin and its rotting treasures that the mad man comes.

Though he must have passed before many times, I imagine I felt him down there, in the street, the first time he came. I felt him that first moment just as I have felt him each time since. So many times.

I rose, as each time I rise, leaving my desk and the pale white paper with its crisp black letters adding up to words which accumulate into sentences without meaning, and turned to my window. Through the glass, deeply tinted against tropical heat, I looked down into the furnace of the street and he was there, standing by the dumpster, watching me.

Yet...I know he can't be watching me. I have stood there in the same spot, with the smell of fermenting garbage squeezing my stomach, and looked up at this window. Adhesive plastic tinting quartered by burglar bars makes it impossible to see anything or anyone inside this office. Even where the shade falls along the ground floor, only shadows float behind the glass. All that can be seen here, on the upper levels, is the reflection of a building across the street and a tiny piece of sky.

But he is watching me, this mad man beside his dumpster shrine. He leans, looking up. He stares directly into my eyes, eyes which he cannot see.

I think of the big container and the steaming garbage it contains as his. I think of the rounds he makes from trash tip to garbage pail to dumpster as a lifetime of pilgrimage.

...A mad man's stations of the cross. The object, certainly, is satisfaction of the body, filling an empty belly. Yet something in his face and in the slow and gentle way he moves makes me think of spiritual comforts as well.

The Fou is naked. No, that is not exactly true. He wears the remains of what, I surmise, might once have been the jacket from some uniform, perhaps the type worn by doormen, or chauffeurs, or even a postman. There seems to be an epaulet. Though I am only guessing, and it is impossible even to guess.

All that remains of the jacket (if a jacket it was) is one shoulder and strips of the collar and waistband. These he keeps fastened with bits of wire, preventing the lump of disintegrating material around his shoulder from sliding down his arm and falling off. Around the wrist of that arm, the last remnants of a cuff, with a brass button, still dangles. The sleeve, between the cuff and the rags clinging to his shoulder, has been completely torn, or has simply rotted, away.

...For the rest, he is naked. If the jacket ever covered the other half of his torso or even his other shoulder, there is not a thread remaining. Unless some small deformity lies hidden by the slight remains of the jacket, he is wonderfully formed. Had Michelangelo sculpted in black marble rather than white, this Fou would have been his David.

He is big, and thickly muscled, and beautifully proportioned.

Yet...there is something unnatural about this body too. The skin, powdered with a fine red dusting of laterite, is as supple and smooth as skin should be, but just beneath it his anatomy is pebbled and hard. It is as though that skin has been slipped over a mould of wood, some magical fluid wood, but still wood. I think his flesh looks like the silicone-treated breasts of the stripper who works the Intercontinental Hotel.

His genitals are huge, or at least they seem so to me. But it's true, the cock and balls are beyond normal dimension. Still, there is nothing grotesque or deformed about them. They are in proportion. He is a very big man, yet I've never before seen a man of any size nearly so well endowed. No man could help but envy him just a little...in this at least.

The Fou is unaware, unconscious of his nakedness, and I wonder why he still wears the remains of that coat. As he paws and burrows in the dumpster I see him grab himself in one hand and shake his manhood to chase off the flies. The act is as reflexive as when he chases the same flies from his ears.

He is neither handsome nor ugly. He has the broad flat face of a southern tribe, but there is no telling which. Just as there is no clothing, there are no face scars to suggest from where he might have come. His hair is clotted in thick twisted dreadlocks with pieces of debris caught up in those knots, but, for the rest, he is curiously...clean?

No, he is dirty, but not excessively so and his appearance is strangely constant. From one day to another, from one month to the next, he is neither cleaner nor dirtier than the last time he passed this way.

This mad man's eyes are bright and aware, but strangely immobile. He looks somewhere far away from this street and the garbage bin.

...Or is he staring at me, safely hidden behind my bars and smoked glass?

He has found a half-eaten mango. Folding the skin inside out he sucks at the remaining pieces of sweet pulpy flesh. Then he eats the skin. Even at this distance I can see the muscles work his jaws.

One afternoon, finding me watching the Fou, my secretary told me that many believe he is very rich and hides his wealth by pretending madness. It is said he owns the big jewelry shop on Avenue Kennedy. It is also said he has healing powers and can see into the future. She laughed when she told me this. She giggled in a way which tried to say she did not want the foreigner to think she really believed such gossip. A hollowness in her laughter betrayed her.

Perhaps it is the future, and not me, the mad man sees standing at this window. But it is my face upon which he rests his gaze.

I have seen him at other times and other places but always, as here, at a distance. I have seen him now and again by the central market and once outside the football stadium. One night I saw him sleeping in the rain at the bush-taxi park, curled against a stack of bald and torn truck tires.

. . . Then, last week, because I came late to work and found my usual parking space occupied, I left my car near the dumpster. As I was leaving for mid-day break, he arrived. I had started the motor but sat there, watching him make his way up the hill toward me and the garbage bin.

He recognized me. The mad man stopped by my open window and stared at me, through me, for what seemed a very long time. He knew who I was. He turned and looked up at my window for a moment before turning his strange far-away gaze back on me. His face was as expressionless as ever and he did not speak. I don't know if he can speak.

There were two baguettes, fresh from the bakery, on the seat beside me. I took one from its newspaper wrapping and, through the window, offered it to the Fou.

He hesitated, then stepped forward a little and took the bread. He turned the loaf in his hands but did not look at it. He was watching me. Then he moved another step forward.

He spat on me.

His saliva spattered just below my eye and ran down my cheek.

Turning away he tossed the baguette into the dumpster.

Janus

HE WOKE IN HIS clothes again. He studied his surroundings through gummy unfocused eyes but saw nothing familiar.

He wasn't alone.

She had hair like hers. Even wooden beads on the braids and those weren't all that common. Her back was turned. She was about the same height, the same build perhaps, even her skin had the same copper texture. The tightness came to his throat for a moment . . . until she rolled over and it wasn't Madeline.

The mind, when sound, is accommodating. It is kind and selective. Hard flinty images are filtered away or bleached and softened through the gauze of nostalgia. Emotions generated by people and events return, but not the people or events themselves. When the mind is sound. Time is telescoped, memories remain, not in isolation, but in the context of events which followed. What has gone before becomes jumbled and blurred.

For Armand the raw nerve of memory could be touched by the smallest thing . . . a snatch of music, the smell of dust, the colour of a market woman's head cloth, the taste of foreign beer, the arrangement of chairs at a café table. A fragment of poorly remembered experience would sheer away and flash across his mind like a brilliant meteorite illuminating in memory every detail of an isolated and often trivial event. Suddenly the mind gave back the past in a way more authentic than the present. The past became present.

Armand's past and present had become so muddled that, lying in the muggy heat of the African morning it required an effort of great concentration to establish with any certainty the country over which this morning dawned and what brought him there. Exactly where in that country he might be and what morning . . . day or even month . . . it was, he had no clue.

Trying not to wake the girl he struggled to pull himself up and cram a pillow under his head. The effort was not a success. He was more uncomfortable than before but did not have the strength to do anything further about it. He was sweating and could smell the rancid odour of his own body. The pain in his chest made breathing difficult. He spotted his lighter and fumbled in the sheets near it looking for cigarettes, eventually managing to find them in the tangle of material. Choking off a cough he succeeded in getting one bent and battered butt ignited. Searching for an ashtray he found, instead, a glass containing two fingers of amber liquid on the tattered rug by the bed. A sniff identified it as whiskey. With one trembling finger he removed a floating insect, mosquito he thought, and in a gasping gulp drank down the burning shot. He tapped the first ash into the empty glass.

The liquor assaulted his troubled stomach and sent acid climbing his throat. He lay very still, swallowing. The burning began to subside, replaced by a warm glow in his limbs as the alcohol hit his bloodstream. He drew on the cigarette and concentrated upon remembering where he was and how he came to be there. Nothing. Where memory of recent events should have been he found a gaping black hole. It was annoying, but not cause for great concern. This hole had been discovered on other early morning excursions in search of memory. In its own time it would fill with at least the essentials if not the details. It must be left to its own processes, whatever they were. One could only wait, patiently. To try rushing these mysteries usually retarded developments and could bring on something akin to panic. Best to steer clear of this empty uncharted region of the mind lest other mental functions, even more important than memory, be sucked into the void which, so often of late, kidnapped recent recall.

He studied the girl beside him for a moment. Attractive in a chunky sort of way but not really very pretty. No clues there. He was certain he had never seen her before in his life, yet here he was in what must be her bed, her room. She was completely naked and he, save for his shoes, was fully dressed. Apparently he had been incapable of completing something lustily enough begun. Like the escape of memory this too was, of late, nothing new. With a shaking hand he brought the smouldering cigarette to his lips. He was thinking idly that he was old enough to know better when, at the thought of age and with an almost audible click, a fragment of memory snapped into place. It was his birthday. Or at least the day before had been, or whenever the party leading him to his present state had begun. He was fifty-six years old. The thought of being fifty-six years old stole whatever pleasure he had felt in discovering the piece of missing memory. He sucked on the cigarette butt, burning his fingers, and stubbed it out in the whiskey glass with a sigh.

A few scenes from the party emerged as from a fog. Madeline had been at the party, he was sure of that. Now he remembered her poking his belly and asking if fifty-six wasn't too old for having babies. It hurt too much to move his head but he studied as much of himself as he could see as he lay. Grimly he admitted that the view was mostly stomach.

The memory told him he had struck her for the jibe. He closed his eyes and threw an arm across his face against the increasing light and returning memory. Too often on mornings such as this, the worst experiences were not finding black holes where memory should be, but the images which slowly and piece-by-piece eventually filled the hole.

The girl beside him stirred. He watched her sleeping and wondered where she had come from and then, correcting himself, how he came to be with her in a place he did not recognize. He speculated on her age, early twenties perhaps, but more likely younger . . . he had three nieces older than that. The body was young and full and firm but there were tell-tale stretch marks across her belly and breasts. She had born a child. Armand wondered what it must be like to be a parent, he wondered who the father of that child might be, he wondered where child was . . . dead at birth or stashed away with relatives in some bush village hacked out of the southern forest. He thought about smoke-filled, mud daub houses leaking rain through rusty tin roofs and concluded it might not be all bad. When this girl was at last too old or fat or just too tired to meet the competition of Yabassi bars she could, and probably would, return to that village and find her place in the household waiting. Old at fifty-six, gone to fat, tired and above all, alone. Where was he to turn? He almost envied the girl that dirt-poor cluster of huts she probably hated. At least in the end she had somewhere to hide.

Outside in the distance a publicity car went by, its loudspeaker blasting music. Armand rubbed a hand over his face and it came away soiled. There was a patch of dried mud on one cheek. He painfully raised his head a few inches and found the knees of his pants and one shirt sleeve caked with red earth. He must have fallen in the roadway or some quartier alley. Then, the more sickening discovery. The dark wet stain of urine across the crotch of his trousers. He touched himself and the grimy sheet and mattress beneath him. Both damp and clammy. Swept by a wave of self disgust he let his head drop back against the pillow.

The self loathing grew. Old and fat and drunk and falling in some muddy street. Pissing his bed . . . no, someone else's bed . . . like some immature two year old. She had made a joke of him, she had laughed and caused others to laugh and, knowing what a joke he had become, he slapped her for saying aloud and to his face what others whispered behind his back. Even with his eyes closed he could see himself, fat as a pregnant cow, hair so thin his scalp burned in the sun, teeth yellow from three packs of unfiltered Bastos Blues each day. She had laughed as they all must laugh. His eyes stung as he fought back the tears.

* * *

Robin leaned against the kitchen counter sipping at his coffee and watched Madeline scramble eggs. In place of her disco dress she had appropriated one of his shirts, the tail of which danced provocatively around her hips as she padded barefoot from refrigerator to stove.

"... all the same, he shouldn't have slapped you," Robin protested.

She made a clicking noise with her tongue and shrugged dismissively. "He was drunk and I made him angry."

"He's always drunk," Robin said. He was puzzled that she should take the incident so lightly.

Madeline laughed. "Yes, almost always drunk. Sometimes a little drunk, sometimes very drunk, but only in the morning is he nearly sober and that is worst of all."

Her good humour was infectious and Robin could not help but smile, "He's a drunk and now he slaps you for making a little joke about that beer gut of his. What is it that keeps you going back for more?"

Passing on her way to the sink she stopped and kissed him lightly on the forehead. "I have two rooms with electricity, a bathroom and a faucet in the kitchen. Armand pays the rent."

"And gets rough when he's drunk . . ."

She paused, for a second. "He's never done that before."

"Well it's a bad habit to get into . . . for either of you."

"It wasn't much of a slap," Madeline laughed again. "He didn't hurt me." She cut two slices of bread and dropped them into the toaster.

Robin examined her long brown legs as she stretched on tip toe reaching into the upper cupboard for a plate. "Seems to me you could do a lot better than that fat old fart."

She watched the toaster in silence for a moment. When the bread popped out she asked, "Is that an offer?"

"I'm far too young for you," Robin countered. "Too skinny as well."

For the first time the easy bantering tone left her voice. "Don't get high and mighty with me my Mr. Robin. Just because I'm making breakfast for you doesn't mean I'm some prize the young wrestler has won by throwing down an old man. I make my own choices and what they are is no business of yours." She swept her hand around the kitchen. "We are not all white in a job with a rich company giving us gas cookers, and frigos, and automatic toast makers."

Robin studied her over the rim of his coffee mug in silence. Suddenly he felt guilty as hell about the refrigerator and pop-up toaster, and very sorry for fat Armand and beautiful Madeline.

* * *

Flat on his back and moving as little as possible Armand patted each of his pockets in turn. Then he repeated the process. No keys. No keys meant no car. What had become of the car? Stolen? No, more likely someone had taken the keys from him and the car was parked somewhere outside a bar or nightclub. He tried to remember who might have the keys or where he could find the car but he confronted the black hole again. He skated away from its depths. Eventually he would find the car . . . and the keys. In time he would remember, just give it a little time.

The realization dawned that he would have to take a cab. He would need a taxi to carry him out of the quartier. Finding a cab meant standing on some township street while gari boys gathered around making jokes in patois and laughing at the white man found lost in the quartier in the light of day. He could hear them chanting:

White man, white man,
With eh long long nose,
Since mah mammie borne me,
Ah neva see dah long nose. . . .

He cringed in anticipation of what was to come. The embarrassment of piss-stained trousers. Humiliation heaped on scorn and shame. Self loathing and disgust mixed with his fear and loneliness. He closed his eyes again and searched frantically for a way out. A way out of the quartier and a way out of what his life had become. An escape from this shoal he had somehow struck.

He felt the girl stir beside him but kept his eyes closed.

"You go die?" she asked.

"Probably," he mumbled, the attempt to speak brought on a coughing fit. His head began to throb and slivers of light flashed across his eyelids. He felt her hand slide along his thigh toward the wetness and pushed it away.

"You are still too drunk?" she tittered, breathing close to his ear and slipping another hand inside his shirt.

He pushed her away again, more roughly this time. "Forget it," he coughed.

"You will perhaps strike me too?" In her voice he could hear the pout. "You came with me, now change your mind. What kind of thing is this? You are what kind of man?"

With a sigh he opened his eyes and reached for his wallet. As the girl watched him frankly, he pulled out a 10,000 franc note and handed it to her. "Will this quiet you down?"

She took the note and folded it. "No jiga-jig?"

"No jiga-jig. Now go back to sleep. As soon as I'm able, I'll get my fat ass out of here."

She looked at him curiously for a moment then turned her back and lay in silence.

He closed his eyes again. She had referred to the incident with Madeline, soon everyone would know . . . if they didn't already. A drunk was no big thing, a drunk falling in the mud was a joke, a drunk striking a girl was an object of contempt. What was said of an old fat white drunk slapping a girl and staggering out to fall in the street he could only imagine. That was how it happened. He remembered now. With hurt and rage turning to shame he had tried to escape. It was raining and the pavement was slick with mud from a construction site nearby. He went down, sprawling. The roar of laughter which rose from the crowded sidewalk tables echoed in his head as another fragment of memory fell into place.

The car had been outside the Tropicana. "How did we get here?" he asked the girl.

"Taxi," she mumbled, already half asleep.

"Where is my car?"

"What car? I no know you get moto?"

"Shit!" he sighed to himself. If his car had spent the night outside the Tropicana it was doubtful it would have tires or a battery by this time. The battered R-4 wasn't worth much but it was all he could afford. Even replacing the tires and battery would cost more than his budget could stand. Painfully he dragged himself from the bed and stood swaying like a tree in the wind.

The girl rolled over. "You go now?"

He nodded.

"I will see you again?"

He stared at her through half closed eyes as spears of pain stabbed along his spine and into the back of his head. "How do I get out of here?" he croaked. "Where can I find a taxi?"

She pulled the sheet up to her shoulders and turned her back. "Go left down the path, past the off-license. There are taxis in the street."

Armand fumbled with the door bolt and lurched into the alley. Shoes. He had no shoes. Back in the room he crawled on all fours to recover them from under the bed. He climbed back to his feet but had to steady himself against the bed post as the pain in his chest returned. When it began to ease he made his way outside and lurched down the narrow track.

* * *

Morning sun played over the table and cast leafy patterns as it dodged through hanging plants and across the balcony. Robin's apartment topped a residential block, which itself stood on one of the many small hills upon which Yabassi was built. Here, even in the hottest season there was always a breeze. Sipping coffee he gazed across the tightly packed mosaic of tin roofs, rusted to a thousand shades of brown and orange and red, broken here and there by the flashing brilliance of sun striking new aluminum. The rhythms of Eboa Lottin drifted from the livingroom stereo. Where the quilt pattern of roofs climbed the next hill, perhaps a kilometer away, the quartier ended in a sharp if irregular line against the bright green of the golfcourse. Above that, atop the hill stood the Mountain Palace Hotel dazzling white in the morning sun.

"Let's go up to the Palace for a swim," Robin suggested. "We could have lunch there and watch the football game on the bar television."

Madeline contemplated the bastion of wealth and privilege isolated on its hilltop above the crowded township and hesitated.

"Look, it's Saturday," Robin went on. "We'll both have friends there."

By some unwritten and long established code the Mountain Palace lowered its social drawbridges on Saturday afternoons. Local girlfriends, never seen on the weekday cocktail circuit, were welcomed as much for the shot of life they brought the otherwise staid and sterile retreat as for the cash spent by their expatriate escorts.

"Armand may be there," she said.

Robin shrugged. She had not said no and that surprised him though this Saturday afternoon Armand would not slouch on a stool at the Mountain Palace bar, he was sure of that. Armand's condition when he left the Tropicana made it almost certain he was unconscious, or at least asleep, wherever he had finally washed up at the high-tide mark of his alcoholic sea. If Madeline wished her night with him to go unnoticed, whether Armand turned up at the hotel or not would not matter. Word would reach him soon enough if they were seen together at the Saturday gathering. She had left the Tropicana with him the night before and appearing together again the following afternoon would prompt the obvious conclusions. Robin wondered what sort of claims Armand felt Madeline's rent entitled him to.

"He's drunk somewhere and you have his car keys. But what if he were there . . . ?"

Somehow she managed to look annoyed and puzzled at the same time. Annoyed by his frown, and puzzled because it would matter little if Armand saw her with Robin. At worst Armand would become surly and threatening, he might even slap her again, but he would not leave her. He might say he was leaving, but it would take little effort to change his mind. She knew that in some way Armand needed her far more than she needed him. She did not understand why this should be and could think of nothing in word or deed which proved it, but she knew it to be true. Armand provided for her and asked little in return, too little. He came several nights each week, sometimes he would visit her rooms every night for several weeks. Yet these were long silent encounters through which he sat drinking steadily and leafing with unfocused eyes through back copies of photo-play romance magazines. She prepared food, gossiped with friends in the tiny kitchen and carried fresh ice to Armand's glass. When the meal was ready he approached it with feigned relish mumbling a compliment as he chewed the first one or two morsels and then lapsed into a sad distant silence again, nibbling a little at the foo foo or njama jama but mostly tracing patterns with his spoon. How, eating so little, he had developed and managed to maintain his massive girth was a puzzle to Madeline.

Those nights when he had drunk too much he stayed at her apartment, sliding often fully clothed into a snorting gasping sleep from which he could not be roused until early morning. On increasingly rare occasions he stayed to be with her but that had happened only four or five times in recent months and each time had been a failure. Only three nights before it had happened again and, in the humid darkness of the night, she had heard him crying. The slap, she knew, came from more than her jibe about his belly. She was a reminder of shortcomings beyond his age and weight.

Most of all she thought of her evenings and nights with Armand as hours passed in a deep well of silence. When Armand was in the house the rattle of pans on the stove seemed muffled, the radio was lowered and conversations with friends were hushed and muted. He did not ask for this, but he brought with him an atmosphere of distant mourning, for someone or something long dead, but still demanding or deserving of respect.

Robin reminded her of what it was like to talk with a lover, to climb out of the silent well. That he talked of Armand and asked impossible questions was troubling, but it was also as if a light had been directed toward that dark and murky corner from which a brooding ju ju watched her every move.

"I must return the keys to Armand," she said.

Robin made no comment. He watched her across the table as she toyed with her fork. She was truly beautiful, one of the most beautiful women he had ever seen. Not just dark and pretty and mysterious in the flattering subdued light of the evening, but fine-featured and graceful and handsome in the flat brilliance of the morning sun. He squinted a little, picturing her with Armand, one hand resting lightly and with seeming affection, or at least loyalty, on his slouching shoulder. He saw her laughing, chattering at the center of a group, then idly sweeping a stray wisp of Armand's hair into place with gentle fingers as he hunched over the bar staring a silent hole in the ice cubes of his drink. The gestures seemed too unaffected, too natural, to be priced at a few thousand francs per

month. Yet, from all appearances, they were. Even Madeline herself had dismissed her relationship with Armand as an agreement,
an arrangement. She puzzled him, she made him curious and with
a sense of revulsion he realized she made him jealous of Armand.
He tried to shake the idea, kill it before it could put down roots,
but it was already too late. He envied fat, drunken Armand.

"He's sleeping it off," Robin said, "but we could leave the keys
with the houseboy."

She shook her head without looking up. "He has no houseboy."

"So just stick them under the door." He tried to sound casual
but it was becoming more important that she come with him.

Madeline was silent for a moment. "What if he's awake?"

Robin wanted to shout, "Screw the old fart! Leave him to his
hangover! Let him waste his own day behind closed shutters, not
yours . . . not ours!" but he held his tongue. Instead he shrugged
and said, "He won't be."

After another long pause she said, "We'll have to pass my room
so I can change?" It was couched as a question, as though she
hoped he might say no, the detour was not possible, forget the
Mountain Palace, go back to Armand.

"We can drop the keys on our way," Robin agreed. He kept his
smile at the small victory inside. "I'll get my bathing trunks," he
added leaving the table.

* * *

Armand saw curious and then grinning faces floating past as he
made his way through the narrow space between mud and cement
block houses. Everyone stared. He was certain everyone watched.
Window shutters opened as he passed, laughing eyes followed his
progress from doorways. At the end of the alley he found the off-
license. He needed a drink. His tongue was swollen and his throat
constricted. The bar had a few low tables in front under a grass
mat sun shade. He went in and took a seat on one of the upturned
beer cases which served as stools. The barman came to the doorway and Armand ordered a beer, then spotting a dusty bottle of
White Horse on an interior shelf, asked for a shot of whiskey as
well. Waiting he lit a cigarette and contemplated his shaking

hand. Only by grasping one hand in the other could he hold the lighter steady enough to touch the cigarette.

"Fever, Patron?" the bar man asked sympathetically as he set down the drinks. "Malaria?"

Armand nodded and, again using two hands, brought the whiskey to his mouth, drinking it off in a single gulp.

"Another," he said handing over the empty glass.

"Five hundred francs, Patron."

Armand paid and the barman went for a refill. Even the quartier bars doubted white men such as he. Money was required up front. He took a swallow of the tepid beer and began to feel a little better. His hands were steadier when the second drink arrived and he drank more slowly.

A group of five young men eating bread and sardines and drinking Guinness sat at the next table loudly discussing a recent football match. They ignored the new arrival but Armand watched them closely, certain they were stealing glances each time he took his eyes away. Pedestrians passing in the street seemed to loiter and watch. He felt exposed and afraid of something he could not identify. There were people standing out there laughing and then they were gone. How had they disappeared so quickly? They were back, and then gone again.

Armand finished his whiskey and chased it with the rest of the beer. He had to find a cab but couldn't face the street. He called the barman and for five hundred francs sent him in search of a taxi willing to carry him directly across the city without loading and unloading dozens of short trippers at every intersection along the way.

It was getting warmer and he was sweating. Again he realized he smelled. He scraped idly at the mud on his trousers with a bottle cap. The dry soil fell away easily enough but a greasy stain remained and always would. The barman was shouting from beside a parked taxi. Armand stumbled to his feet, bumping the table and upsetting the beer bottle which rolled just ahead of his fumbling fingers and smashed against the concrete floor. The football enthusiasts turned silent stares as he scuffled into the street.

As the taxi twisted its way out of the quartier and the whiskey began to settle his nerves, Armand's sense of paranoia eased. Cramps knotted his belly, his eyes stung and fingers of pain squeezed at his neck and head, but the fear was soothed. Yet even though he tried not to, he searched about for one last piece of missing memory. It nagged at him, one interior voice searched for the answer, another telling him it was something he did not want to rediscover.

The cab reached the city center and swung into the principal roundabout. The unfinished skeleton of the new postoffice and Ministry of Communications building rose beside it. Armand studied the building on which he had laboured for nearly two years and the last jagged hunk of missing memory skidded through his throbbing head and snapped into place. Yesterday, after more than twelve years of tearing roads through jungle, laying pipelines across mosquito swamps and throwing up buildings in blistering heat, he had been put on notice. They had been short and blunt. He had overdrawn his sick leave, he had been late too often and had been missing from the site too many afternoons. The company had no place for an old man who drank too much. He was to work out the month, then collect three month's severance pay and a ticket back to France. There would be no references.

The last of the haunting fear was gone, all was remembered.

Arriving at the apartment complex, the driver paused, asking which block he should go to. Leaning forward to indicate the way, Armand saw Madeline emerge from his building and get into a car. He knew that car, and he knew by her clothes that she had not been home. He clenched his teeth and watched her drive off.

The taxi man looked at him. "Patron?"

"Take me back to the new postoffice," he said.

The driver shrugged and made a U-turn.

* * *

The apartment was locked and shuttered. There was no telling whether Armand had made his way home or not. Robin waited in the car as Madeline dashed up the stairs and shoved the keys beneath the ill-fitting door. On the way to the hotel Robin tried to make small talk but elicited only monosyllabic responses from

Madeline as she stared through the side window at the passing
city.

"Look," he said at last, "if you would really rather not go to the
Palace, its okay . . . "

"Armand saw us," she said without turning.

"He was there?"

"I saw him in a taxi as we drove away. Down by the street. He
must have just been getting home."

Robin pondered the new development for a moment. "Do you
want me to take you back?"

"No. We'll have our swim." She spoke so softly he could hardly
hear.

It seemed to Madeline that, at least in the beginning, the
evening had been little different from so many others. Armand
might have been even drunker than usual, though who could tell.
But for the first time in nearly two years she had not gone to his
apartment waiting for him to surface, or gone home, to lie awake
listening for the sound of his fumbled attempts to unlock her door.
Because of the slap? Mentally she shrugged, she did not know.
When he struck her she had stumbled against Robin. There was
no significance in that. He had simply been standing behind her
when the blow landed. Pure chance. Anyone could have been
there, or no one at all. She had been in no danger of falling, just
momentarily off balance, as much from surprise as from the force
of the slap. Robin had grasped her arm to steady her, an instinc-
tive, almost everyday reaction. But then he had turned her a little
toward him, and with his other hand touched her cheek as he
looked to see if she had been hurt. Her face stung but through it
she could feel the gentle caress of his fingers and in his eyes she had
seen both anger and shame at what he had just witnessed. It was
at that moment the night ceased to be like others. Armand had
charged out and into the street. She watched him go, but did not
follow. There was a flurry of concern and sympathy as the group
established that she had not been seriously hurt, but as others
turned back to interrupted conversations and half-finished drinks
she found Robin standing there still, the sadness and concern
showing in his eyes despite a smile on his lips.

Robin swung the car into the Mountain Palace parking lot and stopped. "Okay?" he asked.

She smiled. "Fine. It's hot, let's swim first and eat later."

* * *

The taxi stopped in front of the construction site. Armand climbed out and, for a moment, just stood there seeming to study the layers of ragged posters advertising concerts long past and lotteries no one ever seemed to win, plastered on the plywood hoarding enclosing the new office block. He looked up, trying to see as far as the uncompleted upper floors but the posture made him dizzy and aggravated his lingering headache. He eyed the orange and black sign hung from the third floor windows proclaiming the project to be another example of SATAC Enterprises at work in nation building. He cleared his throat and spat into the litter-choked gutter. Music danced through honking Saturday morning traffic. The Lost Weekend Bar was open. He shuffled off toward the sound. The Lost Weekend seemed an appropriate spot to have one more for the road.

* * *

The Mountain Palace patio was already crowded and noisy. Robin found two pool beds under an umbrella and staked his claim with their towels. Locating a waiter, if possible at all, would not be worth the effort so he went to the bar and brought drinks himself. Madeline was already in the pool chattering with two girls he did not recognize. Stripping to his trunks he stretched out on one of the cots and let the laughter and music sweep over him, but his thoughts were of Madeline and Armand.

* * *

At the Lost Weekend, Armand found a table near the street from which he could watch the traffic and contemplate the soon to be completed Ministry of Communications building. He tossed off a shot of whiskey neat but then settled down to drinking local palm wine. He had spent too much money the night before to afford the luxury of even bottled beer. Palm wine would do just as well, a

little too sweet perhaps, but good stuff. Its effects at least as numb-
ing as distilled liquor, the calm and courage it offered just as effec-
tive as that originating in Scotland's glens.

* * *

Robin closed his eyes and faced himself across twenty years.
Stooped and bent or fat and sodden as Armand. Hair turned from
sun-bleached blonde to dirty yellow straw straggling around a
balding pate. The landscape little changed, tropical hot and green
as the decaying self-exile stumbled a dusty street past staring children and women giggling beneath head loads, pushed to the verge
by frightening rattletrap buses rocketing past in an unfocused
blur.

He saw this old man, chilled, even in the African heat, dying inside, slowly and piece by piece, losing parts of his soul as a leper,
one at a time, lost fingers and toes. Clinging to symbols of life more
than life itself. Symbols like Madeline. The image of the man-to-
come was old at fifty, or even forty, already devoid of life or purpose save that which someone might loan or rent him for a few
brief hours in a steamy gin soaked night. Having already chosen
his grave site he staggered about scraping the hole inch by solitary
inch.

Robin saw, through eyes to come, the camaraderie of the Tropicana and a hundred bars by other names. The lure of laughter and
the rum-fueled fellowship around sidewalk tables as the eddies and
whirlpools of the street cascaded past.

The old man-to-come drifting aimlessly, room to room, through
a cramped seedy government flat, salon to kitchen, to bedroom, to
salon. Splitting, bug-infested bamboo furniture, faded cushions
sagging and torn, hanging through broken slats. Pictures behind
cracked or milky glass, crookedly failing to relieve the cage of
concrete walls. Dog-eared paperbacks listlessly begun and never
finished, tossed upon a dusty shelf of unplaned boards atop crum-
bling bricks.

Escape was to a young girl's quartier room. Smaller and poorer
still, but with the flow of life drifting though it from vibrant rau-
cous allies. The respite, temporary and superficial, that of a spec-

tator, a sham participant, tolerated for the price of monthly rent and market-fund contributions teasingly extorted.

From the pool and patio bar Robin could hear the shouts and laughter of a Mountain Palace Saturday as the equatorial sun poured its heat over him, yet he was sad and lonely and afraid, and chilled to the very center of his soul. For fleeting seconds he had the power of Janus to see, simultaneously, past and future. In his half dream he watched himself chased by the ghost of what might have been toward the specter of what could be.

* * *

Armand retched into the open roadside sewer. He vomited a belly of sour palm wine, spattering his trousers and shoes with stinking milk-white globs of congealing liquid flecked with blood. Unable to straighten he continued to heave but nothing followed the wine. His stomach was empty and dry. He had not eaten for more than thirty hours. Armand wobbled and staggered, nearly slipping on the inch-thick coating of rotted fruit peelings and other slime which covered the sidewalk along both sides of the drain. Retching once more he narrowly missed tumbling headlong into the channel of sewage which lay stagnant but somehow twisting and stretching like the surface of corn boule just as it begins to boil. No one noticed, nor was anyone, Armand included, aware that he had pissed himself again.

Music swept in distorted over-amplified waves from the Lost Weekend and was swirled and mixed and folded within the whine of engines, the blasting horns, the shrieks of skidding tires on asphalt, and the barking, moaning cries which issued from the hunched rocking creature at the gutter as his guts twisted and squeezed in reflexive and futile efforts to expel the residue of too much drink and too much abuse over too many years. The sun was high now and the full power of mid-afternoon heat poured down upon the street, brewing the cauldron of waste in the sewer and broiling the bald aching head and sweating back of the man who stooped so painfully over it.

At last he straightened a little, and once again missing a fall into the corrupted drain by only inches, stumbled into the street. Head down, knees unnaturally bent, arms swinging and clawing air for balance, Armand staggered across the intersection toward the un-finished post office.

Through blind luck, or under protection of those gods who care for drunks, he started his crossing in sync with the traffic light. But before he managed to negotiate even the second of the four lanes the light changed and he became a twisting, turning, bending tree caught in a howling hurricane of traffic. Cars and buses and trucks shot past in a blur of colour, their drivers blasting horns, thumping door panels and bellowing profanities in a mixture of anger and jest. Miraculously he crossed the second lane of traffic and reached the center of the roadway. Vehicles now shot past him in both directions, setting him spinning in his drunken attempt to find escape from the metallic maelstrom. Round and round he went until, at last, he went down. He tried to rise, but couldn't. Kneel-ing in the center of the street he swung wild drunken fists at taxis and motorcycles as they flashed by, howling out his rage and loss, his humiliation and loneliness, in profane unintelligible screams which were swept away unheard in the traffic's roar.

Suddenly, amid cries of skidding rubber, the world seemed to freeze. Armand stared about him confused and shocked. The light had changed again. Someone was pulling at his arm, encouraging, helping him to stand.

"Come, Patron. This way."

He knew the voice but could not find a face to match it. There was a motor scooter beside him but the rider was a woman who studiously looked the other way ignoring him. Squinting he found a cab driver staring down, grinning widely, but it was the wrong face.

"This way, Patron."

He made it to his feet and found the correct face. The gate guard, Simon, from the building site. He followed, lifting his feet with great care and placing them firmly back on the pavement, step by step. When they reached the curb a symphony of vehicle horns rose in salute at the achievement and Armand swung his free arm in a spastic wave of acceptance or farewell. Even as he did so he knew he was playing the fool, the drunken fool making his exit to a fanfare of auto horns.

They passed into the work site through the bent and rusting sheet metal gates he knew so well. Simon ushered him to a bench set against the shady wall of a guard hut.

"Too much mimbo, Patron," Simon grinned good naturedly. "Do you need something?"

Armand tried to focus on the face, the smile marked by missing teeth. The grin seemed twisted and the eyes, he was certain, failed to hide the mockery. "Water," he croaked.

Simon nodded and went off. As soon as he was out of sight Armand pulled himself to his feet again and shuffled toward the building. The ground was broken and uneven and littered with scrap timber, smashed concrete blocks, pieces of tile, coils of wire, and all the residue of a construction project nearing completion. Armand moved with exaggerated care drunkenly picking a path to the freight lift. In a brief moment of lucidity he chuckled bitterly at the thought that he might fall again, among the rubble, and hurt himself. If he were injured, who would care for him? Who would care? He thought of Madeline and his eyes filled. The waste piles of smashed building materials haunted him. Relentlessly, departing from a point he could not recall and along a course of which he had been unaware, all his useful pieces had been cut away, used up, bit by bit, day after day, year after year, until all that remained was a chunk of broken, splintered misshapen man, cast off and dumped with debris too useless even to be carried off by the African laborers to find a final simple usefulness in the shanties of the township. He thought again of Madeline and faced with finality that, like the dirty rotting timbers around him, he was past usefulness even in the quartier. Sweating with effort he slid open the lift gate and lurched inside throwing the power switch and pulling the up lever. The lift did not, as yet, reach the roof but for Armand it went far enough.

Eight floors above the street it was strangely quiet and a breeze swept the structure passing unobstructed through open space between the floors where walls were yet to be built. In the shade of the thick concrete ceiling it was cool and pleasant. Armand walked to the edge and, with hardly a pause to contemplate the pile of rubble waiting to embrace him, stepped off into space.

A Day in the Life

THE AIR CONDITIONER vibrated in the wall, its grumbling punctuated by sharp snaps and pops, but the room was hot and humid as a steam bath. He knew without looking the machine had turned to a block of ice, its coils and vents frozen solid.

Jay lay staring at the ceiling, willing himself to get out of bed. There would not even be the temporary relief of a shower this morning. Water service had been cut back to three days each week now. Though clouds hung over the city like dirty, mouldy, cotton wool, promising an end to the dry season, they brought no rain, only humid heat.

He had not slept well. Laying naked atop a single sheet he had tossed and turned, haunted by senseless dreams and brought fully awake by even the smallest noise.

He dragged himself off the bed and dressed in yesterday's clothes. After a sleepless sweaty night and no morning shower he could see little point in a clean shirt. The whole office would smell of unwashed bodies this morning.

For long minutes he stood contemplating the near empty interior of his refrigerator. There were a dozen beers and a soda but nothing edible. Even if there were, he doubted he could summon the energy to prepare it.

He slammed the door. If he left immediately he might still find a parking place near the Porteur Cafe.

* * *

"There was shooting around the Presidency last night . . . early this morning actually."

Godfrey rattled his newspaper. His glasses were pulled low on his nose and he squinted over them at the fine print of the football scores. He was probably sixty or more but he didn't look older than fifty. Though his hair had passed grey on its way to white, his deeply tanned face was that of a much younger man. "I didn't hear it."

"It was gunfire," Jay assured him, "I'm sure."

"Probably was," Godfrey agreed.

The younger man dropped three sugar cubes in his coffee and stirred, waiting for further comment on his news. Godfrey reached one hand around his paper and broke off a piece of croissant. He popped it in his mouth and chewed, his attention still riveted on the sports scores.

"It must have been a coup . . . or at least an attempt," Jay prodded.

"Must have been," Godfrey agreed.

Jay watched a group of four market women, fat and sweating, their enormous enamel pans of trade goods at their feet, haggle loudly with a taxi driver. Their kabas were all of different colors but printed in the same pattern. A huge image of their President for Life's paternal smile spread across their broad behinds. The insanity of the morning traffic seemed no different than usual.

"There was nothing on the radio news this morning," Jay added.

"Never is," Godfrey grunted.

That was true. Daily headlines amounted to an item or two about the cocoa harvest or some similarly compelling subject and an appeal by one Minister or another for discipline, hard work and national solidarity. Added to these items of supposed local interest would be a wire service report on a Brazilian bus plunging off a cliff or an Indian ferry going down with massive loss of life . . . the more massive the better.

"Nothing in the paper either?" Jay asked.

"Never is," Godfrey repeated.

The street noise increased a decibel or two. A government car had rear-ended a taxi and another loud argument had broken out. As the two drivers, out of their cars now, volleyed verbal abuse back and forth their lower legs seemed to dissolve and reform in heat waves rising from the asphalt.

"It's eight in the morning and the heat is killing me," Jay grumbled.

The weather seemed to interest Godfrey even less than gun fire in the night and he made no response.

"I suppose," Jay ventured again, "if it was a coup attempt it must have failed?"

"Maybe," Godfrey shrugged, turning to the back page of his paper.

"So who's president?" Jay laughed, but there was a sense of frustration in the sound.

"Who knows?" Godfrey said. "The old goat hasn't been seen or heard from in nearly a year has he? This isn't the first night there's been shooting around the big house. Maybe we've had a half dozen Presidents in that time." He pulled the stub of a pencil from his shirt pocket and began working the crossword.

Jay watched him for a moment. "A pre-schooler could do that puzzle, for God's sake."

"A retarded pre-schooler could do this puzzle," Godfrey laughed pencilling in the boxes.

Jay tried again. "So who's running the country."

"Nobody."

"Since when? Since last night, or since last year?"

Godfrey looked up from his paper for the first time and grinned. "Since forever."

Jay smiled back at the older man. "You're a cynical old fart. Someone has to don't they? I mean the alternative would be chaos?"

"Exactly," Godfrey agreed, nodding toward the stationary snarl of taxis in the street. All movement was now completely blocked at the intersection where the traffic light hung like a suicide on its wires over a stalled truck. A dozen push cart vendors had become entangled in the cars and motor scooters which were trying to find a detour along the sidewalk.

"But that's the beauty of it," he went on. "It may not be neat and clean and tidy, or in straight lines, but at least there's no one telling us what to do. God help us if some 'strong man' type ever wins one of those shoot-outs on the hill and tries to impose order on all this. We'd have to go home." He went back to his crossword, squinting over his glasses. "Chaos is, after all, the natural human condition," he added.

* * *

"Have you seen Jacobsen's field tour report?"

Olsen looked up at Jay sweating in his office door and flipped the pages of his own copy where it lay on his desk. "Got it right here." Long damp strands of colourless hair hung across Olsen's watery eyes and his red complexion seemed even brighter than usual. He carried at least a hundred excess pounds and seemed to suffer the heat more than anyone else. Taking a swallow from his coffee cup he made a sour face. "Damn janitor reheated yesterday's brew again."

"Does Jacobsen know what he's talking about?" Jay asked, thumbing the pages.

"Yup. He's been around forever and seen it all. This he's seen a dozen times. He knows what to look for and how to interpret what he finds."

Jay shook his head. "This is a full blown disaster. He says if food relief doesn't reach Guider within thirty days we can expect at least a thousand deaths in that area alone. Do you think it can be as bad as all that?"

With some difficulty Olsen propped his feet on the desk and turned slightly in his chair so he could look from his window into the embassy parking lot below. The splash of water, as drivers washed cars, could be heard faintly over the hum of his ineffective air conditioner. "It's worse. They're already dead."

"Already dead."

"Ignore that date on the cover page and check out Jacobsen's travel dates."

Jay leafed through the first few pages. "This is six weeks old!" he exploded. "But I just got it this morning!"

"Me too," Olsen nodded. He unbent a wire paper clip and began picking his teeth.

"Where has it been?"

"Oh, you know, making the rounds."

"Making the rounds? What rounds?"

"Well, Jacobsen had to get back from the bush and write it, that took at least a few days. Then his Division Chief made about six hundred changes and Jacobsen argued with him over it for a few days . . . though of course he finally gave in and re-wrote it. That took another day or so. Then, the same thing happened several times over because it had to pass the Program Officer and the Ag Officer before it ever got to the Deputy Director for forwarding to the Director. We can't forget that, somewhere along the way, it sat on a desk for a week or so because someone was on leave . . . and that each time a change was made it had to be completely retyped, and we all know the speed of secretarial services we have in a country where the manual typewriter is considered high tech."

Jay opened his mouth to speak but Olsen waved him off.

"So, when at last it got to the Director, it was already a month old and a thousand people were dead . . . with probably a couple of thousand more on their last legs. This unhappy fact no doubt got the Director to thinking about possible political repercussions so he decided the Ambassador should see it before he gave a final clearance signature. Of course, the Ambassador too has advisors so . . . well, you get the idea. It's been making the rounds."

"Jesus! You're telling me more than a thousand people have starved to death while a simple field trip report was going through channels?"

Olsen picked up his cup and slopped its contents around but didn't taste it again. "Yup, that's what happened. But to tell you the truth, I'm surprised it saw the light of day at all. In a way, I rather wish it hadn't."

"Something like this could be buried!?" Jay asked, incredulous.

"Misplaced, more likely. Sit down will you. All your twisting and turning and arm flapping is getting on my nerves. You're making me sweat just watching you."

Jay sat.

"Doesn't it strike you as odd," Olsen asked him, "that none of our local government counterparts have been around here crying the blues about drought and famine and holding out the old begging bowl?"

Jay tossed his copy of the report on Olsen's desk. "Now that you mention it, I guess it does."

"I thought it might," Olsen nodded, finally mustering the courage to take another swallow of coffee. "Well," he choked, "I, for one, don't find it strange at all. Those cases of terminal malnutrition up there are not the President's people . . . so to speak. In fact they have, from time to time, in both word and deed, expressed profound disrespect for the old dictator. I doubt His Excellency regards the present situation in the Northern Provinces as being so terrible as you do. Quite the contrary I should think."

"That's genocide!" Jay protested.

"Genocide is, I believe, the word for it," Olsen agreed.

"Well, what are we going to do about it? What about this new emergency food bank thing?"

Olsen dropped his feet back to the floor and began searching through the papers on his desk. "Got there ahead of you on that one young man," he said, finally retrieving what he was looking for. He held up a computer printout. "We have . . . sorghum and rice at Galveston, milk powder in a couple of great lake ports, vegetable oil at some New Jersey dock I never heard of, and there's wheat somewhere on the Mississippi south-bound for New Orleans. It's all just waiting for a Call-Forward order."

"It's spread over half the North American continent!" Jay said, shocked. "None of it is any closer to Guider than six to eight weeks . . . hell, this is only March, that stuff in the lake ports is still frozen in!"

"Good point," Olsen nodded, pulling a pen from his drawer and scribbling on the print out. "I hadn't thought about the St. Lawrence being iced up."

"That's what they call a food bank!?"

"What did you expect? Did you imagine we had the stuff stacked up in the embassy warehouse?"

Jay sighed. "So what about getting a Call-Forward?"

"You know as well as I do, that process begins with a request from the host government and we've already agreed they haven't exactly been storming through the halls screaming 'famine'! This is also a regime with which we maintain 'friendly and fraternal diplomatic relations,' Jay. As such, we do not interfere in its internal affairs. Didn't they give you the 'mind your own business' lecture at Foreign Service School?"

"Oh I got the lecture, but what it means in this case is that there's no drought and nobody dying at Guider unless that clown on the hill says so."

"Very nicely summed up. You have a bright and promising diplomatic career ahead of you, my boy."

"Cynicism runs rampant," Jay sighed.

"And not without reason," Olsen grinned.

"So what does it take to pry an appeal of the President?"

"He has to decide he has more to lose than he has to gain by starving these people to death."

Jay tilted his head, curious. "What are you getting at Olsen?"

"Well . . . this government can't be embarrassed, they don't know the meaning of the word . . . but ours can. This government can, however, be pressured or even threatened and, sufficiently embarrassed, our government is capable of arm twisting from time to time."

"What are you suggesting?"

Olsen shrugged.

"The press?"

"Speak softly, softly."

"The media doesn't even know where this rat-hole is."

"Don't be dull. Famine, with a nice touch of heartless scandal . . . especially if the word genocide can be used . . . is good news wherever it comes from. Reports like Jacobsen's go astray all the time. Leaks are the modern mark of a true participatory democracy."

Jay leaned forward, resting his arms on the desk. He lowered his voice but spoke with enthusiasm. "We could do that! We could do something important here, for once . . . break this paper log jam and probably save a lot of lives."

"We?" Olsen asked, arching his eyebrows. "I've been sucking the government tit for seventeen years. I've no intention of being weaned at this late date. I'm making payments on a retirement place in the islands."

"God, man! Lives are at stake here, thousands of them!"

Olsen went back to picking his teeth with the paper clip and said nothing for a long moment. "You know what I've discovered? I've learned that one death is a tragedy. A hundred deaths is a disaster. A thousand deaths, or ten thousand deaths . . . those are statistics."

Jay was stunned. "You're quoting Eichmann!"

"Am I?"

"You must be kidding!"

"The truth, Jay, just the truth."

"Well if you won't help I'll do it myself." Jay stood angrily grabbing his copy of the report from Olsen's desk.

"Good for you Jay. A brave and noble decision. Just remember, when they come around asking how that report turned up in the Washington Post I'm going to tell the truth, the whole truth, and nothing but the truth . . . so help me God." Olsen turned back to the window to see if the drivers had started washing his car yet.

* * *

They lay for a long time, silent, sweating from their lovemaking and from the close airless weight of the room. A branch of the mango tree outside scraped against the tin roof and Jay thought perhaps the window curtain moved a little. Maybe a breeze was rising, maybe the rains were coming at last. The day, like every day for weeks, had been hot and humid and he looked forward to the rain. It would come soon, Lissette had told him, any day now.

Do you love him?" Jay asked.

"Who?"

"Reiner, for God's sake!"

"He's a very kind person, but he is very young."

"That's not an answer."

She rolled over, turning her back to him. He contemplated the long tapering lines of her body, flowing from the strength of her shoulders to the delicate narrow waist and swelling again to buttocks as round and firm as the young mangos ripening on the tree outside.

"It's not my business, I suppose, but this is pillow talk...just between us," he explained. "Don't be angry."

"I am not angry," Lissette laughed, but she did not turn back.

"But you have accepted? You will marry him?"

"I will marry him."

"But until you go off to join him, you will sleep with me?"

"If you want."

He wanted. But he wanted something else too, something more, though he could not identify what it was. "Have you ever been in love?" He kept his tone as light as he could. "You know...stupid, blind, passionate, irrational love? Like in the photo-play magazines or the cinema?"

"Have you?" she asked.

"Yeah."

"How often?"

Jay laughed. "Just once."

She pushed herself onto her back again. "Have we any cigarettes left?"

He fumbled in the damp tangle of sheets and found the pack. He lit one for each of them. "So, have you ever been really in love?"

"I guess not. Who was she...your one true love?"

"You're mocking me."

"No I'm not." She kissed him lightly on the cheek. "I'm just curious, like you. Was she white?"

Jay took a deep drag of the cigarette. "We were students. We were going to get married after graduation." He watched the curtain but could not be sure if it was moving or if it was a trick of the shifting light from the oil lamp.

"And...?"

He was still watching the window curtain. "One day she stepped into the street without looking...right in front of one of those big Checker Cabs you see in American films."

"She died...?"

"Before she hit the pavement."

"I'm very sorry." Lissette turned her head a little on the pillow and watched his profile for a moment. "I guess I don't love him. At least not the way you mean. He's so young."

"You said that before," Jay reminded her, "but he's the same age as you?"

She lifted an ash tray from the floor and set it on her naked belly. "Yes, but he lives with his family in that small town with the funny name . . . Kochl am See, that's it . . . and he has seen little. He had never been away from Germany until he came here to visit his friend. Life has not yet shown him its teeth. He is very young."

Jay reached over and tapped off an ash. "And you are no longer young . . ." It was meant as a question, but it sounded as much like a statement.

"Now you are mocking me."

"No I'm not, but you too are only twenty-six."

"I am a woman. I left my father's house when I was fifteen. I had a child when I was seventeen. That child died of fever in my arms as I searched in the rain for a taxi to carry us to the clinic. I buried my child on what should have been his second birthday and while I was already carrying another in my belly. I have been hungry, I have slept more than one night in a police cell, and I have passed a good many nights in places much worse than a cell." She lit another cigarette from the butt of the first. Jay said nothing, there was nothing to say.

"When I talk of age," she went on, "it is not of years, but what those years contained. So he seems young and, yes, I am old. And he . . . and you too . . . with your innocence and your talk of love, make me feel older."

Jay closed his eyes. "I'm sorry, I guess you have certificates from another school. I just meant you are still a beautiful young woman, that life can still offer . . . "

"Look at me," she said softly, reaching out and turning his face toward her. "Look at me carefully. I am just wise enough to know I am getting old. Look closely. Look around my eyes, see the marks the babies left on my belly, feel the fat inside my thighs. My feet and hands are turning to leather."

"No, Lissette, you are beautiful . . . the most beautiful thing I have ever seen."

"You see what you want to see."

"No . . ."

She dismissed him with a laugh. "You should have known me last year, or the year before."

"You will always be beautiful."

"No I won't. Time alone takes that away, and the kind of time we have here takes it away very quickly. I have two, perhaps three years left . . . in which to decide. I still have one child I must think of. You may be right, life may still offer possibilities, but can I take that chance? Dare I wait for this love you talk about? . . . I will be his wife as he asks."

"Do you at least tell him you love him?"

"No."

"I think you should. It may be as you say and he is much like me. If so, I know he will need to hear it."

"Yes. I want to tell him, but I can't make the words pass my lips."

"Life has taught you so much, but you don't know how to lie?"

"Of course I can lie. I'm an excellent liar. I've just never had to lie about that before. It never mattered."

"It does now. You had better practise."

She laughed. "Yes, I suppose I must practise."

"You can practise on me. Tell me you love me."

She just laughed again.

"Tell me," he repeated.

"I love you," she whispered.

"A lie if I ever heard one. Try again."

"I love you."

"A little better, but a long way off the mark yet."

"Please, Jay, leave me be."

"Go on. Tell me you love me . . ."

* * *

The rains had not come. The air, still and stagnant, wrapped around him like a damp glove. He pulled the door closed and stood for a moment watching the leaves of the big mango tree, seeking any hint of movement. There was none. Only the lower branches were visible in the small arc of light cast by a weak door bulb across the alley. They hung limp and sodden with heat and spoke, he knew, for the whole giant tree . . . and perhaps the whole world.

A dog chained at the door of a hairdressing salon raised its head as he passed down the narrow path but it did not bark.

Along the main road he found the sidewalk littered with sleeping bundles. The whole quarter had abandoned airless rooms seeking a degree or two of relief in the open air.

Jay looked up. There was no moon and there were no stars. The sky spread above him was a heavy black velvet shroud. It seemed so low, so close, that he reached out, imagining for a moment he could touch it.

Wrist Watch

SHARP GUSTS OF damp wind snapped at a poorly fastened poster, causing the heavy paper to crack and pop. In the glare of a street lamp across the road, Liengu could see rain mist hang suspended in the night air. The pavement was already a glistening dark mirror throwing back distorted reflections of the street lamp and garish lights on the cinema marquee beneath which she stood. Through the exhaust fumes of thinning traffic and the smoke of soja braziers at the corner she could smell the heavy scent of an approaching downpour.

Even as she dug in her bag, pulling out the zippered case once meant for sun glasses but now serving as a change purse, she knew the effort to be pointless. Dumping its contents into her hand she found two buttons...one red, one white...a single plastic earring, three aspro tablets in cellophane wrappers and seventy-five francs. Just as uselessly she stirred the other contents of her bag but, though she turned up a mate for the ear ring, there were no more coins.

She sighed, submerged in a wave of despondency coloured by growing anger and resentment. A taxi to the camp cost one hundred francs. The bus, smelling of rotted fruit beneath the seats and unwashed bodies, jammed with rowdy boys who pinched and grabbed, cost twenty-five francs and required joining a pushing, shoving crowd now gathered on the unsheltered side to the street. She pulled her sweater closer and chastised herself for not carrying an umbrella.

Liengu shivered and looked at her watch, not to know the time, because time really didn't seem to matter, but to marvel at the ironic absurdity of the watch itself.

The watch was, certainly, the most beautiful time piece she had ever seen. Its graceful feminine lines sat on her wrist, deep golden tones glowing in the light of the arcade against the soft dark warmth of her skin. Delicate Roman numerals on its face sparkled through the sharp clarity of its crystal. The watch itself sat suspended in an oval of gold which in turn was held to her wrist by another, heavier loop of gold, snapping with a solid, almost comforting, sound into the suspension loop. The watch was, all at a time, beautiful, clever, carefully crafted, and very expensive. She knew, now, just how expensive because, by chance, she had seen the same watch in a shop window that afternoon. The tag, small and discreet, showed a price equal to just over three times her monthly salary. One quarter of her annual earnings.

She stood, buffeted by the growing wind, staring at the watch and pondering the insanity of a situation which saw her wearing a piece of golden jewelry equal in value to three month's income, yet at the same time unable to afford a one-hundred franc cab fare.

Contemplation of the watch fed the despondency, the encroaching discouragement. Despair that even as a teacher, after so many year's service, she should earn so little. That her salary for a month equalled only one-third the price of such a watch. That she should find herself having spent only five hundred francs to see a film and be left with less than cab fare in her purse. Eight year's service to a Ministry she served only under contract since, even after those earlier years of study, the degree achieved went unrecognized because it came from a University in another country . . . a neighbouring African country, but another country just the same. After another twenty year's service, what then? What would her monthly salary buy? Would she be able to see a film and still afford cab fare? Unlikely. Just as her contractual employment today condemned her to half the salary and none of the benefits enjoyed by even lesser qualified colleagues, so at the end, there would be no pension or continuing benefits.

Challenged, the director of personnel had told her bluntly that

young women did not attend university at their own expense.
They attended the national university on a government scholar-
ship or they did not attend at all. They most certainly did not
study in another country. Those who claimed to have done so
brought back diplomas earned with their bodies and not their
brains. The director explained these things as though to a child, a
recitation of well known facts. As for government assisted housing
and future pension benefits these were reserved for those with
legitimate diplomas and therefore recruited into the cadre of the
official civil service. Furthermore, women did not require such
benefits, women married men with diplomas and positions within
the cadre and enjoyed the benefits earned by their husbands.

Miss Ekema was thirty-four years old, the director noted flipping through her file. Why was Miss Ekema, beautiful as he had to
admit she was, still unmarried? Liengu had said nothing but that
had not stopped the line of enquiry. It was well known, the director had gone on looking up from the file, that Miss Ekema had a
white boyfriend. Why then should she be concerned with salary
and housing and other benefits with a white man to pay the bills?
Was her white man so lacking in generosity as to refuse buying her
a house, or at least renting an apartment? Did he care so little as to
see her without pocket money? It was well known, the director
conceded, that the white man in question was already married
which might explain why she showed some concern for her future,
but was this man so lacking in affectionate concern that he could
not see her set up in her own house, and a business perhaps, before
he went back to his own country, as all white men eventually did?
The director saw no reason, he said, why Miss Ekema, possessing
an obviously fraudulent diploma and with a wealthy foreigner to
see to her needs, should take up his time with interviews concerning imagined injustices at the hands of the Ministry. Miss Ekema
would do well, he concluded showing her the door, to thank fortune that the Ministry faced a shortage of teachers or she would
have no employment at all.

Every time she thought of that interview Liengu was overcome
by shame and rage and helplessness mixed in equal proportions.
Lately a new emotion was seeking its place among these . . . each

day that had passed since the agony of the interview she had felt the approach of surrender.

In the aftermath of that futile attempt to seek justice, in her humiliation she had constructed a dozen imaginary scenarios in which she had all the right responses, all the clever retorts to throw back at the director. She rewrote the meeting in a form where she showed the man how tradition-bound, how foolish, how absolutely stupid his position was, how "bush" his attitudes showed him to be, but she knew these victories existed, and could exist, only in her imagination. The director, however much she wished to deny it, represented the way things were and she, in her struggle to make it on her own, represented a silly imaginary world which did not, and probably never would, exist.

Even told the truth, men like the director could never believe let alone understand. Her "white man," as the director called Joel, was quite prepared to provide the help suggested, but she had refused. She had refused many times over. She had refused so often that even her relationship with Joel, which she had tried so hard to build on love and love only, had become strained, as he sought ways in which to show his affections, and was now little more than a hollow shell of what it once was, or had at least shown promise of becoming. For more than two years she had watched Joel's struggle to give her tokens, tokens she would not accept, in place of what he could not give . . . himself.

The strain had, in time, been too much for him and now he had become sullen and empty, sleepwalking through the motions of a relationship he no longer believed in. She had imagined she would find in Joel, a European, a man who could understand her drive to be her own person, her need to achieve at least those small successes of life as an individual. Yet it seemed he was still a man and, though for different reasons, could no more accept her drive for self achievement than could the director.

Just as Liengu saw the bus approaching, and prepared to dash across the street, the rain arrived in force. It slashed down the roadway in slanting driving curtains of wind-driven water. She stepped back against the theatre front, seeking shelter in the doorway, and watched her last alternative to walking home come and go.

The battle, she had to admit, was becoming too much. The tasks she had set herself had seemed, over the years, noble and right and the constant defeats had about them an air of honour. This in itself had provided the strength necessary to go on for so long, but the feeling of struggling in a good, even though self-defined, cause was no longer enough to sustain. Leaning there in the cinema doorway Liengu had to admit that she was weakening fast. She was tired of the fight, she was tired of losing, she was tired of the gossip, she was tired of the contempt shown by people like the director, she was tired of being alone even with the man she loved, and she was tired of being poor.

She looked again at the wrist watch and asked herself why she fought when it could be so easy? Why go on struggling when soon it would be too late to seize other opportunities offered? She was thirty-four but, as even the director had conceded, she still had her looks. That was how it was done. That was how one avoided nearly a decade of hard work without advancement or without hope of security at the end of two more decades just like the first. Why walk home in the rain for want of cab fare when even a car was possible for so little effort? Why live in a pigeon hole of an apartment when a villa could be had so easily?

Liengu removed the watch from her arm and studied it closely. A wrist watch costing three month's salary and to obtain it she had only asked the time. The speeches of congratulations for the new Minister had gone on for so long that she idly wondered how late it was . . . concerned, as usual, about finding a cab. Seated beside her at the reception the man in the colonel's uniform had laughed when she asked and teased her about having no watch. The next day a corporal arrived at her school, driven in a Peugeot 504 with national security number plates, and delivered a gift-wrapped package containing the wrist watch with a card bearing only the Colonel's name and office address. The Colonel's ability to locate her so quickly came as no surprise considering the registry of the car and the address told her he too must be married.

Such approaches were not unusual, though in this case the value of the gift was. Still, as always, Liengu had not responded. Nearly two months had passed and she had heard nothing further from the Colonel. At least he had been a gentleman about it and there had not been the unpleasantness of constant harassment as was too often the case. Yet she had frequently wondered about a man in a position to give a gift of such value without putting more effort into enjoying some sort of return on his investment.

She had showed the watch to Joel and told him how she received it, hoping the incident might stop his silent slide away from her but he only shook his head and said nothing. Though she often caught him staring at it when he thought she wasn't looking.

The rain continued to pound the street in torrents and Liengu contemplated selling the watch. With the proceeds, if combined with those of her djangi due in a month's time, she might manage a trip to Dakar to buy dresses and material for resale to friends and colleagues. The profits, if she were clever, could set her up in a small business which, with nurturing and a little luck, might put her sufficiently on her feet to quit teaching in a year or so and allow her still to build a future on her own terms. The idea lifted her spirits momentarily but then she realized such a venture, even if successful, would condemn her to several more years of near poverty, of standing in the rain without cab fare.

Joel, even now, would be willing to help launch the project if asked, but she knew it was too late. She could not ask because it would tie them both to a relationship already as dead as her dreams of independence. She was tired of trying to build something from nothing and she was tired of being poor.

Though she tried not to think of it, there was another course of action open. Her uncle had found a man for her to marry. A man of good position, a customs inspector, but a man of nearly sixty years, already once a widower, and fat and ugly in the bargain. Her uncle had gently pointed out that a woman of thirty-four could expect little more, all her age mates already having found wives, but she had refused. Even the hopeless grind of teaching for another twenty years at a pauper's wage was preferable to that.

Deep in her misery, wrapped in the slashing sound of the rain, Liengu did not hear the car pull to the curb.

"Excuse me," the voice asked, "but do you have the time?"

Liengu looked up and found the dark Peugeot parked in front of her. The rear window was rolled down and the Colonel smiled at her. "I see you have a fine watch there, I do hope it keeps correct time?"

"It keeps time very well," she agreed, clipping the time piece back on her wrist without looking at it.

"Could I drop you somewhere? Home perhaps? This really is a very bad storm and the taxis all seem to disappear at the first hint of rain."

The Colonel spoke to the driver who jumped out into the storm with an umbrella and came to Liengu's side. She stood for a moment contemplating the scene and then looked at her watch.

"It's just a bit past ten p.m.," she told the Colonel.

"Then perhaps it's not too late to stop somewhere along our way for a drink, something to warm you on such an unpleasant night."

Sheltered by the umbrella Liengu went to the car. The driver opened the door and she slid into the warm interior beside the Colonel. "Yes," she agreed, "perhaps a drink would be nice. It's so cold out there. It seems I've been standing alone in the rain for years."

Eight-Bar Love Affair

"*Je suis en train de tomber amoureuse de toi.*"

"What?!" He understood her, and the statement spoken in a breathy whisper near his ear demanded a response of some sort, but taken by surprise he was at a loss.

"*Je deviens folle de toi.*"

"I don't believe this," he groaned, only half aloud but she heard him even above the over-amplified music.

"Is true," she affirmed, switching to English and pressing her warm musky body closer. "Feel how my heart beats." She took his hand and pressed it on her small firm breast.

They swayed a little to the French ballad blasting around them. With their feet planted firmly on the gritty floor the embrace could hardly be described as dancing, but as the lights went down and, from somewhere in the darkness she had touched his fingers, the invitation had been to dance. He neither accepted nor declined, he had simply been pulled by a firm but small gentle hand from his bar stool and into the pack jamming the floor.

"What are you called?" Her voice had a rhythmic sing-song quality about it.

"Chris," he said, then realized it might have been better to lie. Too late.

"Chris," she repeated, trying the English pronunciation on her tongue. "I am called Catrine."

He said nothing.

"My name is Catrine," she said again.

"Pleased to meet you, Catrine," he mumbled looking about desperately for Michael. The club was too dark, the only illumination coming from two far off red lamps. Somehow he felt he needed rescue, but just why or how he hoped Michael would assist him was unclear.

She sighed pushing her thighs and pelvis against him. "I love you," she breathed again. He felt himself begin to stir.

They shuffled on until at last the music faded away. He began gently to disentangle himself from the girl's embrace, trying desperately to get his bearings in the dark. The door, the toilet, somewhere to seek peace and a moment to think. But the lights did not come up and the fading ballad blended smoothly into a new tune, as slow and sweaty as the first. The girl hung her arms around his neck, her lips breathing close by his ear slid across his cheek and brushed his own tentatively and gently. He took a deep breath.

"Yes," she sighed, "and for me as well."

"Jesus!"

She giggled. Her hand traced fleeting patterns up his spine and caressed his neck. In spite of himself he found he was holding her closer and his own hands were slipping to the small of her back and lower.

"You are from where?"

He swallowed hard. "Winnipeg."

"My region is Mbalmayo," she told him. He was sure she could have no more idea where Winnipeg was than he did of where Mbalmayo might be, but he wasn't about to press the issue. She slipped one leg, ever so slightly between his. Maybe he should have lied about Winnipeg just the same.

"Chris, do you think I am pretty?"

"I haven't even seen you!" The statement burst out in a tone of confusion and despair.

In his arms the girl's body trembled with laughter. "But me, I have seen you. I have been seeing you for some time." She hugged him to her and softly kissed his neck. He could feel his palms sweat and his mouth go dry. He was terrified, embarrassed, and the growing warmth in his groin hurt a little. She pushed against him.

"We can go somewhere?" she whispered in his ear.

He tried to tell her no, that he had nowhere to take her, but his tongue stuck to the roof of his mouth and his throat constricted. His mind wanted to say no, but his body would not let him. Then the music ended.

"Thank you . . . " he gasped and, as the lights came up with the beat of a Makossa rhythm, stumbled his way through the throng of dancers. A stab of panic sent his hand searching for his wallet but it was still there. Spotting Michael in a booth he scrambled in that direction and flopped, wild eyed, onto the bench beside his friend. A touch on his arm turned his head.

"Would you offer me a Fanta?" the girl's voice asked.

It took him a moment to make the connection between the soft ups and downs of that voice and the girl smiling beside him. "Oh shit . . . you're beautiful . . . " The tone of desperation didn't belong with the statement, but desperation it was.

"Tu est gentil," she murmured dropping her eyes for a moment. Then she stopped a passing waiter and ordered her drink.

She was truly lovely, deep shining bronze, intricately braided hair, tall and slim, wearing a red fringed disco dress which was in only mildly bad taste.

"Oh shit," he said again.

"Introduce me to your friend," Michael prompted.

"Catrine, this is Michael. Michael, Catrine." They shook hands.

The waiter arrived with her bottle of Fanta, no glass, no straw, and it was warm. Chris paid the equivalent of twelve American dollars for it.

"I must go and tell my cousin that I am leaving soon," she announced and darted off into the crowd.

"Very nice," Michael commented. "Known her long?"

"Don't be stupid."

"She seems to like you."

"Like me!? She says she's in love with me!"

"You work fast."

"She works fast! The lights went out, she dragged me onto the floor, the music started and eight bars later she says she's falling in love with me! My God, even in four four time that's fast!"

Michael grinned and took a sip of his drink. "If I were you I'd just be thankful it was me she fell in love with. She's gorgeous."

"Be serious. The girl's a prostitute."

"A harsh word, Chris, a very harsh word."

"What would you call her?"

"I think you said her name was Catrine."

He said nothing for a moment, eyes darting over the crowd but she was nowhere to be seen. "She wants to go home with me."

"Well she is in love with you after all." Michael kept a straight face but his eyes were laughing.

"I can't take her with me! Dave's in the next room, he'd be horrified . . . I'm horrified. I can't go home with a whore!"

Michael clicked his tongue. "Another very crude and inappropriate word."

"Inappropriate?"

"You're a long way from Winnipeg."

"That much I've discovered for myself. I don't believe you Michael, would you actually sleep with a girl like that?"

Michael lit a cigarette and took a deep drag. "She loves you and she's beautiful."

"I'm serious," Chris protested. "Would you . . . have you . . . actually slept with a girl like that?" When he said "like that" the element of distaste in his voice was evident.

"Never one quite as lovely as your Catrine."

One part of him said he was behaving like a farm boy come to town, another part was amazed and even shocked that Michael, the same Michael who had grown up on the same block in the same Winnipeg suburb, whose parents had played euchre with his own in alternating over-heated kitchens every Wednesday night, who had been in the same Boy Scout patrol at St. Andrew's United Church, who had played with him on the same minor hockey team, who had even taken his own sister to their high-school junior prom, could possibly have slept with a girl like Catrine. " . . . A harlot??!"

"Where do you get these words?" Michael asked, finally laughing aloud. "The King James translation of the Old Testament?"

"You're laughing at me . . ."

"No Chris, I'm not. I'm laughing at your vocabulary."

Much the same thing Chris thought, embarrassed. Twenty-eight years old and a woman was scaring the hell out of him. Worse still he was letting it show in front of his best friend. Where had she gone to? He searched the club again but didn't see her. The Fanta still sat on the table. He found himself hoping, just a little, that she had not gone home. "Don't you ever catch anything?"

"Catch what?"

"You know what I mean . . ." he was making a fool of himself again.

"Why do you think Dr. Fleming spent all that time mucking about with mouldy bread?"

"I heard it's penicillin resistant."

"Dr. Fleming's successors came up with Tetracycline."

"Antibiotics don't cure AIDS!"

Michael slumped down on the bench. "You've got a bad mouth," he groaned. "Prostitute, whore, harlot, and now AIDS. Stop talking like that or I'll wash your mouth with soap."

"Michael, AIDS kills!"

"Do you know what AIDS stands for, Chris? Appalling Invention to Discourage Sex, that's what. We're here for a good time, not a long time. Besides, somewhere one of Dr. Fleming's torch bearers is on the threshold of a breakthrough."

"That's not what the newspapers say." Now that he had thought of AIDS he was getting really scared. She had kissed him.

Michael took a swallow from his drink and stood. "Well, in the meantime we have to make do with rubbers, don't we? Now I'm going to find some soap for that mouth of yours." Climbing over Chris' legs he disappeared into the crowd.

For a moment Chris thought of making his escape, just slipping away and lying low until his plane took off in less than forty-eight hours. Then he realized Michael had the car keys and he had no idea where he was or how to find the hotel. He was also somewhat surprised to discover he wanted to see a little more of Catrine before he went to ground. He tried to balance his established image of girls found in bars like the Caveau and the reality of Catrine's charms, then the warmth of her lips was on his neck again.

"How do you do that?" he gasped.

"Do what?"

"Appear out of thin air! One minute you're nowhere in sight and a split second later you're kissing me."

"I love you."

It didn't seem much of an answer, but she spoke as if it were. He let it pass.

"How old are you?" He was trying to make conversation, partly to keep her from kissing him, at least so long as the lights were up, and partly to prevent her from darting off again. As soon as he asked he realized how uninspired and plain dumb it sounded, but some sort of talk seemed called for and in his turmoil it was the best he could manage.

"Oh," she replied in an offhand way, "twenty . . . or maybe twenty-two. How many years have you?"

"Don't you know how old you are?"

"My mother did not register my birth at the Prefecture until I was big enough for school. Then she could not remember if I had been born the year before President Sadou was shot, or the year after." She laughed and the sound was music. For the first time he laughed as well.

"Do you have a big family?" He had heard African families were, by Canadian standards, huge. The question wasn't all that inspired, but it was an improvement over his last conversational gambit. Although he was not fully aware of it he was becoming curious, and even interested, in this, to him, remarkable young woman.

She slid closer to him and laid a casual hand on his thigh. Her smile seemed almost shy. "Oh no, I have just one child . . . a boy." There was a hint of pride in the announcement that it was a boy.

He stared at her in disbelief and wondered at the same time why the discovery that she was a mother should leave him slack-jawed and speechless.

Filling his silence she asked, "Are you married?"

He shook his head.

"Do you have any children?" she continued.

He shook his head again, still mute.

Michael reappeared, with a very tall, very black girl in tow. As the girls greeted each other in some local language Chris whispered hoarsely to his friend. "She's got a kid!"

"Remarkable," Michael commented, his eyebrows going up. "She doesn't sag a bit . . . boy or girl?"

"Michael! She's a mother," he hissed. "I'm being hustled by somebody's mother!"

The girl squeezed his arm and he turned to find a waiter, tall beyond belief, with a head shaved completely bald and totally devoid of ears as if the razor had taken them as well, bending stiffly over their table. "Do you want another drink?" Catrine asked.

"By all means," he stammered. Even at twelve bucks he definitely needed another drink.

"Me too," Michael called from the rear corner of the booth where he huddled with the tall girl. "One more round and we'll get out of here. It's two a.m. already."

"Where are we going?" Chris asked, panic rising.

"Where I'm going you're not invited," Michael grinned. "I presume you have your own arrangements anyway?"

"I've got no arrangements. What are you saying? What am I supposed to do? I don't even know where we are!"

Michael shrugged good naturedly. "You're a big boy. The street is full of cabs. Get in one and tell him Hotel Sanaga. Of course if you really intend going alone it may not be as easy as it sounds."

Chris sat for a moment becoming more entangled in a web of confusion. Then, jumping to his feet, he announced, "You and I need to take a piss."

Michael looked puzzled but followed him through the club to the toilets. In the men's room Chris spoke after some hesitation. "Now I know you probably think I'm some kind of wimp but . . ."

"I don't think you're a wimp," Michael chuckled laying a hand on his friend's shoulder. "I was new here once too. The trip to Africa is a lot further than a few thousand miles."

Chris grinned, a little relieved but still uneasy. "Well look . . . what I want to know is . . . I mean . . . I mean do you actually pay a girl like Catrine to sleep with you?"

"Heavens no!" Michael assured him.

"You don't? No money changes hands?"

"Now I didn't say that . . . "

"Michael?"

"Look Chris, Catrine out there has probably been to elementary school for four or five years. I'm willing to bet at least one of her parents is dead, she comes from a bush village somewhere and has left behind more brothers, sisters, cousins, aunts, uncles and other relatives than you could count. She tried to escape that village but at least once a week those relatives take it in turn to come here and 'borrow' money for medicine, school fees, taxes, and things you and I could never imagine including paying the ju-ju man to lift evil spells off the manioc patch. There are no jobs here for anyone, least of all some girl who didn't even finish grade school and she almost certainly does not have the right family connections within the power structure. Five days a week she probably sells Makra beside the street or earns enough money through some other buy-em sell-em enterprise to pay the rent and eat. She may even be somebody's house servant. But on Fridays and Saturdays she scrubs down in a basin of cold water, borrows a little make-up from a friend, puts on her best dress and comes here."

Michael paused and lit a cigarette, contemplating, then he went on.

"She comes here mostly because, the way things have turned out, this as close as Catrine will ever get to the life she thought she was escaping to and, in a way, you represent that life. I suppose it's also obvious she hopes to go home with someone like you who, with luck, will be kind in the night and generous in the morning . . . not payment, Chris, a gift, a contribution to the market fund. A gift because you find you really like her, and she likes you, and you want to help a new friend. Even if you were to leave nothing there would be no argument from Catrine . . . disappointment on her part no doubt, but this isn't Winnipeg, she's not going to call her pimp. It's not like that."

Chris stared for a long moment at his friend. "You're completely full of shit, Michael," he said at last. "I've never heard such a crock of romantic bull-shit in my life!"

Michael grinned widely. " . . . but isn't it a much sweeter view

of Catrine than your 'whore,' 'prostitute,' 'harlot,' stuff. . .
bitter-sweet at least. Besides, there's as much truth in my 'crock of
romantic bull-shit' as there is in your biblical adjectives."

"She comes on pretty strong for the girl you've just described,"
Chris reminded him. "She says she loves me."

Michael smiled again, a little wistfully. "She's using a vocabulary learned in the cinema and from cheap romance magazines. It
just doesn't mean to her what it sounds like to you."

"I'm sorry, Michael," Chris said, after letting his friend's story
sink in for a moment, "but it still sounds rather sordid to me."

Michael sighed, "There's another of your hard words. But I
suppose, from a point of view, it can seem that way. We choose our
perspectives."

"Just as an academic question, how much would you 'contrib-
ute' to the market fund?"

"Tempting, isn't she?"

"I didn't say that," Chris protested, but to himself he had to
admit there was an attraction.

"Oh, five or ten thousand francs . . . it depends."

"Depends on what?" he pressed.

"I don't know man . . . if you like her, how drunk you are . . . it
just depends." Michael tossed a cigarette butt in an odorous uri-
nal.

Chris sighed, "Well, I'll just have to take your word for all of
this, but for me Catrine is a journey too far in too short a time."

"Yeah, I can see that. It's no big thing you know. You're behaving like some kind of obligation has been dumped on you. You've
got nothing to prove to me, we've known each other too long for
that."

Chris relaxed a little. Michael was right. He was carrying on
like a teenager. "That just leaves the question of how I give her the
slip. Has this place got a back door?"

"No back door. Very cavalier attitude toward public safety in
these parts. Just go out there, make up some lie sufficiently outrageous to save face for both of you and give her a couple of thousand
francs for cab fare. She'll pout a little, but everything will be
okay."

"You sure?"

"I'm sure."

"What should I say?"

"Give her a variation on the truth. Like you said, Dave's in the next room at the hotel, just enlarge a little. Tell her your wife is back at the hotel."

"I already told her I'm not married."

"Silly boy . . . Okay, tell her you're sharing a room with your mother."

"What!? She'll never believe that."

"Of course not, but she'll pretend to. It's better than either of you having to admit you don't want to sleep with her. After all, she's in love . . . she has her pride . . . and apparently so do you."

Chris sensed an edge in his friend's voice. "I'm not faulting or judging you, Michael," he said. "What you said may be true. It's just . . ."

Michael smiled, a little sadly perhaps, and moved to the door. "Of course you're not. Your visit, tonight in particular, has just reminded me of how that clear spectrum of bible belt morals tends to bleach and fade in the African sun. Come on, gentlemen never keep the ladies waiting."

The girls were still seated in the booth, chatting in patois and sipping warm Fanta.

"We go now," Michael announced. The tall girl joined him and they shook hands with Catrine and Chris. "See you around somewhere, sometime tomorrow, mate," he told Chris. Catrine looked expectant and Chris looked edgy.

When they were alone he sat on the bench again and the girl joined him. He told her about his mother and the difficult accommodation arrangements. That she did not believe him was obvious, but as Michael had predicted she made no protest.

"You could come to my room," she suggested.

Once begun, he stuck with his story. "My mother is expecting me, I'm very late already." That piece of fabrication made him feel like a highschool kid again. "She's not well and I should not have left her alone for so long," he embellished. Then he gave her two thousand francs. "For the taxi."

She slipped the bills into her purse. "You are very kind. Will I see you another night . . . tomorrow?"

That one caught him off guard. "Ahhh . . . well . . . yes I could try to come tomorrow night," he lied again.

She smiled but he wasn't sure she believed him. "I will wait for you."

"I must go now," he said, and in spite of himself leaned over and kissed her cheek.

She squeezed his hand. He stood to go but, for a moment, gripping his hand, she held him back. When her fingers relaxed he turned and, with more reluctance than he cared to admit, made his escape.

Although he would recount events of the next few minutes many times, and dissect them in his mind over and over again, exact details never came into focus. He was preoccupied with the girl, he was perhaps a little drunk, he was in strange surroundings and the door lamp of the night club did little to relieve the darkness. Climbing the stairway to street level he passed someone coming down, the doorman perhaps but he was never certain.

After the roar of the club, the silence outside was deafening as he paused to take a deep breath of cool early morning air. The road was empty and the cluster of taxis which had jammed the curb at midnight were gone, though a few meters to his right, where the narrow street sloped up toward the main road he could see one of the battered yellow vehicles parked near a huge trash bin. He made his way, a little unsteadily, toward it.

As he reached for the door handle, bending down a little, a stunning blow, low on the back of his neck sent his head crunching against the door frame. Pain shot down his spine and, head spinning, he lost his balance, sinking to his knees on the gravel. A powerful hand, bunching his shirt, jerked him back to his feet and dumped him on his back across the trunk of the car.

"*Ta porte-monnaie!*" a voice growled.

He felt something poke his cheek. Willing himself back to semi-consciousness he opened his eyes and looked down (or was it up?) the blade of a long, crudely made knife into the very ugly face of a huge assailant. The knife point was stuck into the skin of his face less than a millimeter below his left eye. He may have found much about his African visit strange and foreign, but he knew a mugging when he saw one.

He felt the vehicle beneath him rock, heard a door open, a shout, and then watched his attacker exchange angry and threatening words in patois with someone out of sight behind him. The taxi-man, probably sleeping at the wheel, had been awakened by the scuffle. It also seemed he had been effectively warned off.

"Patron," the driver's voice called unsteadily, "give your money. He says he will blind you if you struggle . . . "

Keeping his eyes riveted on the robber, he moved his right hand with slow deliberation, reaching down and beneath himself to his hip pocket. In order to free his wallet he was compelled to roll his body slightly to the left. Giving him room to do so, the mugger removed the knife from his cheek and lifted it an inch or two away from his eye. Just as Chris felt his fingers touch the wallet the face above him broke into a screaming cry of surprise and pain. The dark form of the taxi driver came hurtling past him as the knife fell against his chest and rolled away clattering against the metal of the car. His attacker disappeared from view.

Stunned, scared and shaken he managed to regain his feet. Disoriented by the blow and the darkness, it took a few seconds before he could fully grasp the scene before him. His attacker lay face down on the ground with the cab driver kneeling over him. Even in the poor light he could see a thick stream of blood leaking from a ragged gash in the back of the skull, soaking the thin cotton shirt and forming a dirty pool by the limp, unmoving shoulder. Standing over the two men he discovered Catrine, a blood-spattered high heeled shoe held at waist height as if at ready should a second blow be called for.

The driver spoke rapidly to the girl. He stood, glanced up and down the empty street and searched hurriedly in the night until he found the knife. Placing the weapon back in the thief's hand, he turned to Chris. "Maybe he go die. We move." He opened the rear door of the cab.

Catrine still stood over the bleeding body, shoe in hand. She looked puzzled. Chris stepped over the prostrate form on the roadway and touched her arm. She reached down and removed her other shoe, walking barefoot to the taxi. As they climbed in, the driver took the bloody shoe from her and wiped it clean on the mugger's shirt. Then he tossed it into the rear seat after them, closed the door and hurried around to his place behind the wheel. As the cab shot off up the hill, Chris looked through the rear window. In the darkness he could not be sure, but there could have been a shadow standing in the doorway of the nightclub. His hands trembled and his head ached, but, for some reason, inside he felt very calm.

The taxi, old and very noisy, rattled and banged its way along broken potholed streets. Over the racket the driver shouted to Catrine a question of some kind, and she responded at length. The cab roared on, turning left, turning right, turning left again, through dark and unfamiliar streets. Chris sat watching the night-wrapped city lurch past them and wondered, only casually, where they might be and where they might be going. He slid across the seat, a little closer to the girl, and took her hand.

"Are you hurt?" she asked. The musical rhythm was still in the voice. The tone calm and soft as when they had held each other dancing in the crowded club.

"I'm fine. My head hurts a little, but it's feeling better now . . . you're an amazing lady. You probably saved my life."

She didn't say anything for a moment and though, when she spoke she sounded confident, there had been a tenseness in her silence. "I don't think so. He would not have killed you."

"From my view of events it certainly looked like he might cut me up," Chris said.

"That, he might have done. In this city there are some very hard people. Life can be very difficult and people are sometimes badly hurt . . . but seldom killed."

He recalled what Michael had told him in the men's room, and began to see the imaginary life portrait his friend had tried to sketch in a new and shifting light.

The taxi swung into a hard U-turn, crossing the dirt road, and stopped on the opposite side. The street here had been cut into a hillside. From his window Chris looked out across the dark rusty corrugated roof tops of a quartier lying well below them. "Where are we?" he asked.

"Home," she told him, opening her door and climbing out. The cab was parked so close to the falling shoulder that he had to slide across and follow her out the opposite door.

She was paying the driver and he leaned down at the window as well, pulling ten thousand francs from his wallet. "You have been very kind," he told the cabby, offering the bill. "I can never repay you for your help . . . "

The taximan pushed the money away. "I have been paid for my fare. All I beg is, if anyone should ask, if the police should ask, about tonight, that you do not remember me or my car."

Chris nodded. "Of course. That is the least I can do. Just the same . . . " He pushed the money toward the man again only to have it refused a second time.

"I was not at the Caveau tonight. None of us saw or heard anything in that street, Patron." He put the car in gear and drove off, one pale tail light disappearing into the night.

Chris watched the taxi until it was gone.

Catrine spoke behind him. "His brother-in-law's sister is married to a cousin of my uncle's senior wife. He is not from my village, but he is family." She handed Chris her shoes. "Please carry these for me. It rained yesterday and the path is very slippy."

He took the shoes. "He was helping you, not me." It was a statement more than a question.

Catrine pouted. She led him to the edge of the embankment and slowly they descended a long flight of muddy steps hacked into the red earth. At the bottom, they entered the quarter, the ground continued to fall away in front of them, a much gentler slope, but steep enough to make walking on the greasy laterite awkward and at times treacherous.

The houses were a mixture of mud block, ill-fitting clapboard, cement and corrugated iron, built so close together that all light was blocked out and at times they had to skid along single file, Catrine holding his hand and leading him blindly through the maze. After what seemed a confusing eternity of stumbling twists and turns, she stopped at a door, barely visible in the darkness, and took a key from her purse.

Catrine's room was small. It was so tiny that after the addition of a double bed, a clothes rack, and mirrored dressing table with a

miniature bench, she had to move about sideways, squeezing past
furniture.

Though the floor sloped badly, it was of concrete and a strip of
fraying carpet covered the narrow space beside the bed. The sheet-
metal roof was tight and did not leak when the rains came. There
was a ceiling of woven mat, mounted on lath frames, to insulate
the room from a tin roof scorched by the sun. Ceiling met walls ir-
regularly and tipped slightly in a direction opposite the run of the
floor, but both the mats and the lath had been varnished and the
effect was not unattractive. The walls were of mud brick, thick and
cooling even in the hottest months. Though outside, the one-story
house was coated only in banco daub, the interior had been inex-
pertly plastered with a thin layer of cement and painted white with
a green band at ceiling and floor. By design or otherwise this
matched a fading green spread covering the bed.

On the wall hung three calendars, all of different years and none
current. One was illustrated with a portrait collection of Nigerian
State Governors, another with the photos of the Cameroon armed
forces senior command and the third, the largest, a picture of a
French chateau with sweeping vineyards in the foreground. There
was also a small photographic portrait, in a heavy frame, of her
family. Father dressed with obvious discomfort in European
clothes, suit jacket and tie, seated in a straight-back chair, gripping a walking stick, his two wives in traditional attire flanking
him. Three frozen black faces staring rigidly into the camera.
Finally, above the bed, a roughly carved crucifix.

The room had electric light but, turning up a storm lantern, she
explained the service had been cut off for non-payment. One tiny
window, no more than twelve inches square and glassless, would
let in a small patch of light when the wooden shutter was opened,
if the day was dry, not too hot or not too dusty. For other days, and
long evenings without electricity, the hurricane lamp sat at one
corner of the dressing table.

An interior door, of three unplaned boards hung on heavy
hinges, led to a larger room, long and narrow. At the end closest to
Catrine's chamber was a two-seat couch, occupied by a curled and
sleeping girl of about twelve, and three chairs of cane grouped

around a low table decorated with an embroidered cloth under a vase of plastic and paper flowers. Beside the chairs, on a folding cot, slept a little boy clutching a headless toy dog in a tiny fist.

The opposite end of the room served as kitchen, well enough appointed with a tabletop gas cooker and a small kerosine refrigerator. An open cupboard, its sides and door covered with mosquito netting, contained a few boxes and packages and cans of food while a limited collection of cooking pots hung from nails driven into the mud wall above.

Catrine woke the girl who rose, studied Chris curiously for a moment, and went out into the night. Catrine locked the door behind her and pulled a fallen sheet over the child. "Can I get you anything? I have some aspro."

He rubbed the back of his neck and nodded stiffly. "Yes, a couple of aspro might help."

She carried the lantern to the kitchen area and rummaged in the cupboard, eventually coming up with a packet of tablets. From an earthen jug on the floor she dipped a glass of water and handed them to him. "Let me see?"

He swallowed the pills and bent down so she could examine his neck. She touched it gently. "You've got a bad lump, but it has not been cut." As he straightened up she pulled his face to her and kissed him long and softly on the mouth. This time he responded without second thought, with affection and with passion.

A lifetime of acquired values were suddenly turned upside down and banished; found unsuitable for export and returned, unopened to their manufacturer. He pulled her soft yielding body to him, feeling it mould itself around his own rising in warm desire. Her tongue darted, exploring, within his mouth, then pulled away. She lifted the lantern from the cupboard top and walked, careful not to wake the child, toward the bedroom. Drawn, he followed the yellow pool of light.

With flowing movements, but cool deliberation, she undressed, carefully placing her dress on a wire hanger and hooking it on the clothes rack. Here there was no sweaty, clumsy fumbling through blind embraces for deviously concealed hooks and buttons and zippers. He followed her lead. She slipped her pants down long bronze legs and tossed them in a wicker basket, neatly replacing the lid. He folded and placed his own clothing on the dresser bench.

Any imperfection there may have been in the beauty of her naked body was masked by the soft lantern light and the shifting shadows it cast as the flame danced in the small draft of their movements. She turned down the bed but lay, one knee raised, arms behind her head, atop the sheet. The night was warm and the air in the tiny room still and close. He lay beside her, propping himself on an elbow, studying the smooth ebony perfection of her face. Leaning over he kissed her forehead.

"Your mother, by now, will be truly vexed," she said running a hand softly along his injured neck.

He watched her closely for a moment, and then the teasing smile came. Rolling together in a close embrace they laughed.

As they explored each other with gentle slowness, he discovered a woman who lay with him for her own pleasure and needs as much as for those of her partner. Catrine brought him an awareness that the temperate women of his experience, bred and nurtured in central heating and introduced to physical affection in hopeless grope sessions, tangled in layers of winter clothing, sprawled on sub-zero rear car seats, had been givers only. Cooperative and willing, perhaps, but still non-participatory partners. Somehow the suspicion always lurked that a duty was being performed. Performed gladly and even lovingly, but in the end, a duty.

Catrine gave. She reached out and gave him pleasure and joy far beyond the reaches of his imagination, but she also received. She showed no hesitation to guide and lead. No reticence in taking her turn at orchestration or picking up the conductor's baton.

Light was leaking around the shutter edges when, at last, they slept. It was only in the final moments before sleep claimed him that he wondered, for a fleeting moment, if what he had experienced had in fact been real or, if after all, he was just the farm boy taken in and fooled by a tropical land and the wiles of the women it bred.

"*Amoureux,*" she whispered. "I love you Chris."

The sound of his name, accented by her voice, chased away all attempts at reconciling old lessons with new, and held at bay all questions. They disappeared, riding night shadows as they fled before the rising sun. Nor did he think of a body, bleeding in the dirt.

He was awakened several hours later by the sound of a child's voice. The little boy, standing on tiptoe to see his mother behind Chris, was speaking excitedly.

"There is someone at the door," Catrine explained rolling over him and reaching for a wrapper cloth on the clothes rack. "A white man."

As she tied the cloth high over her breasts he stumbled from the bed and started dressing. The little boy stood staring at him with frank, wide-eyed curiosity.

In the salon he found Michael looking tired and drawn. "It seems you've had quite an evening," he commented. The tone was light enough but he did not smile.

"Would you like coffee?" Catrine asked.

Before Chris could respond Michael accepted. She went to the other end of the room and busied herself at the stove.

"How did you find me?" Chris asked.

Michael dropped his voice to a near whisper. "It took a little doing. That girl I was with knew Catrine and I took a chance you had changed your mind. I've apparently been a little quicker than the police . . . about an hour after we left the club they turned up at my house looking for you. Seems they found a body outside the Caveau with a great bleeding hole punched in its head. They say they have a witness who saw this guy fighting with a white man who matches your description. Does any of this sound familiar?"

Chris' eyes darted toward the kitchen and found Catrine, standing stock-still, staring at him. "No," he said after a moment's hesitation, "this is all news to me."

Michael shrugged. "The fucker was a known thief and a violent one at that, but he's dead just the same and the whole city is in a flap. Worse still, it's you they want to get their hands on. Whether I believe you or not doesn't matter much, we've got to get you out of here." He reached in a pocket and pulled out an air ticket. "You're reserved on the UTA flight taking off in ninety minutes. Forget the luggage, the police are at your hotel."

Chris sat frozen, completely at a loss. Struggling to get his thoughts in order, he finally said, "They'll have the airport covered too..."

"Very likely," Michael agreed. "But I pass people through there several times a week for the agency. The booking clerks and airport police see me around all the time. I have an expense account from which I tip generously. There's a lot of procedure and security but it's all very sloppy. If we keep moving and keep talking we might make it. At the airport they aren't likely to know the man they're looking for is associated with me."

Again Chris hesitated, confused, trying to grasp what his friend was telling him. Trying to come to terms with murder on top of everything else that had happened in the past few hours. Watching Catrine again, he asked, "What if I turn myself in? This is a misunderstanding of some kind, couldn't we straighten it out?" He saw the fear in her eyes.

Michael shook his head, "Don't you even think about it."

After another long pause he took a deep breath and said, "My passport and wallet are in the other room." Catrine followed him inside and closed the door.

Leaning limply against its rough panels she faced him across the narrow space at the foot of the bed. "Thank you Chris." He shrugged and forced a crooked smile.

"I mean it truly. All you have to do is tell the truth and everything will be all right...for you," she added.

He reached out and touched her face. "You said you loved me." Through the fear and confusion knotting his stomach he managed to force a smile of ironic humour.

Michael shouted from the salon as she put her arms around his neck and kissed him. "Goodbye," she whispered. "I will beg God to watch over you. I am so sorry..." He pulled away, reluctantly, and left her standing by the dressing table.

From Catrine's house to the final departure lounge events unfolded very much as Michael had predicted. They drove in silence for many minutes until Michael asked, "She came up behind that hood and took him down with a spike-heeled shoe, didn't she?"

Chris looked across at his friend, surprise betraying him. He started to speak but decided, once again, he had nothing to say.

Michael turned his eyes back to the road having found the answers he sought in the lengthening silence. "For what it's worth," he said at last, "I'm with you. You're in deep shit, but there's no point sacrificing her unless we have too."

Chris turned to Michael, startled, but at the last moment bit his tongue and, once again, said nothing.

At the airport Michael took his passport and tickets. Darting in and out of offices, laughing, hand-shaking, talking, back-slapping and dropping a blizzard of five-thousand franc notes, he processed him into the International Departures Lounge with practised skill. They shook hands at the glass doors in a tense farewell.

With less than thirty minutes to flight time Chris was beginning to relax and then the police came.

He was escorted to a glass-paneled office and told to sit. One of the officers sat across the room and the others left. Nothing was said, no questions asked, no explanations given. Fear spread growing tentacles from his knotted stomach, wrapping themselves around his chest and constricting his throat. The faint trembling in his hands could not be controlled. Creeping from his bruised neck fingers of pain began to poke and squeeze about his head.

The pre-boarding announcement crackled over the speaker system and through the glass he watched passengers gather their hand luggage and form a line at the exit. Fighting down panic and despair he willed himself to sit quietly as his eyes searched that part of the outside foyer where Michael had been waiting. He was nowhere to be seen.

First-class passengers were called to the big blue and white DC-10 on the apron, still he waited, under silent guard. The remaining travelers were told to proceed to the plane and filed into the sunlight. The police officer sat unmoving, without comment. There was no sign of Michael.

He waited, listening for the whine of jet engines taxiing away without him but there was only the hum of the air conditioner and the sound of his own laboured breathing. Time seemed to have lost all dimension.

The door opened and another policeman entered, an officer. He spoke in patois to the guard and left. The guard stood, "Come with me."

Taking Chris firmly by the arm he led him through the lounge and onto the tarmac toward the waiting plane. Overwhelmed by confusion he stumbled forward. Looking up, over his shoulder, he searched the faces on the viewing deck. Had Michael, somehow, at the last moment managed to perform or buy a miracle. He was still nowhere to be seen. As they neared the boarding stairs a feeling of joyous relief swept away the horror of the previous half hour. Reprieve, against all odds, had been achieved. Once more, squinting through the glare of midday sun, he searched the crowd atop the terminal. Michael was not there. Then he froze. Near one end of the gallery he saw her, Catrine, watching him. On each side of her stood a police officer.

His escort, tightening his grip, pushed him forward. He struggled, trying to turn back, but the police guard twisted his arm painfully behind his back and shoved him roughly onto the steps. As he fell and lurched back to his feet there was a shout. The guard pulled him around and there was Michael, with another policeman, the officer, walking toward him carrying his suitcase.

"It's okay, Chris. As you can see they're letting you go. I even managed to get your bag. Calm down . . . "

Chris's eyes darted back to the viewing deck. "Catrine . . . ?"

Michael shrugged. "I had to give her to them. At the last minute they realized who you were."

"Gave her to them?"

"It was your ass or hers. I had to make a deal."

"Michael, you don't know what happened. She saved my life. Tell them. I have to stay to explain, testify . . . "

"A white man in a local court? Don't be a fool, Chris. You'd both die in jail . . . probably before there was any sort of trial anyway. Besides, the deal has been made and a deal is a deal."

"You just traded her for me!?"

"She's a whore, Chris, you said so yourself. We managed a cheap enough price. Now get on the plane."

"Last night you wouldn't even use the word, Michael! You said there were no whores!" Chris protested.

"At night there are no whores. Look around you, it's hard daylight now, Chris." Michael nodded to the policeman and they dragged Chris up the ladder.

Puppets

THE OLD MAN coughed, the spasms becoming progressively worse until they ended in a retching heave. He spat into a piece of crumpled newspaper and examined the result. He knew the blood would be there. His interest was only in how much.

In a month's time Benjamin Ojuka would be sixty-eight years old and, on the day his country marked only its third decade, that seemed old indeed.

A plastic radio, dusty red and cracked, sat at his elbow sputtering and popping out the family announcement program. There were occasional congratulatory messages concerning marriages and school graduations but, for the most part, the announcer laboured through endless calls for family members to gather at funeral celebrations. All of the deceased were younger than Benjamin Ojuka. At least one in three was a child.

Benjamin recalled his own daughters, both dead within weeks of their birth. He thought of a son taken by meningitis when he was twelve and of his wives buried these many years. Two other sons and a daughter, living in Canadian exile, were alive only in the technical sense. For Benjamin, they were further away than their siblings and mothers. At least the graves were close enough to visit. When the time came, Benjamin thought, it would be a sad funeral celebration indeed. A man is shamed to have no wife or children to mourn at his graveside.

He stirred a little condensed milk into his tea and coughed again. The announcements were replaced by a blast of brassy martial music heralding the 8:00 a.m. news broadcast.

"... Thirty years ago today," the announcer began in somber tones, "the freedom loving peoples of Karamoja threw off the imperialist yoke of colonial domination and stepped from the dark shadow of racist oppression into a bright dawn of liberty..."

Holding his saucer carefully beneath his tea cup, Benjamin rose from his chair and crossed the narrow room. He stood at the window looking down into the rutted alley known as Acacia Street.

The provisions shop facing him was open in defiance of a Presidential Decree ordering that no business be transacted on this day of national celebration. As a small concession, perhaps to the date or the decree, one of the paper flags distributed to school children had been planted crookedly in an open rice sack on the stoop. The shopkeeper stood in his doorway speaking to someone Benjamin could not see in the shop beneath his room. The radio droned on.

"... Imposition of an inappropriate and unjust constitution having failed, we, the sons and daughters of Karamoja, suffered two decades of despotic oppression at the hands of ruthless dictators. Reactionary opportunism exceeded even the cruel stupidity of the imperialist regime..."

Benjamin smiled sadly. That was a point of view even he could share.

"... But in our darkest hour, a new sun rose in the east. Gathering about him a cadre of dedicated and politicized followers, a lone patriot began building our Movement of National Salvation. Through the trials of bush war the MNS gathered strength and marched from victory to victory until the second liberation of Karamoja was achieved.

"... Today we celebrate our independence twice over, and salute the achievements of our Saviour..." Benjamin snorted and bitterly recited along with the announcer, "... His Excellency President Lieutenant Colonel Josa Bida Andanha, Chairman of the Movement of National Salvation, Commander of the Heroic Armed Forces, the Great Equalizer, Senior Son of the Motherland, Father and Husband of the People, First Depositor of the Karamoja Development Bank..." There was more but the old man reached down and turned off the radio.

In the silence he could hear a siren wailing. The National Saviour himself would not be on the move as yet, but Benjamin could picture Presidential Guard units racing their Land Rovers at reckless speed up and down streets long since closed to public traffic. The point of all this high-speed, high-decibel dashing about was never clear. Nothing more, perhaps, than the theatre of the occasion.

The scream of sirens and roaring engines came from Nile and Zambezi Streets, the route the Senior Son of the Motherland had chosen to follow from the Presidential Palace to the Square of the Unknown National Martyr.

On his daily outing to buy a newspaper and drink a cup of tea at the Speke Grill, Benjamin had yesterday gone two blocks out of his way to watch the prisoners, in their denim shorts and singlets, sweep the gutters and whitewash shop fronts along Zambezi Street. For the past six years he had made it his habit to inspect these preparations, not because he had any interest in the set dressing itself, but because he thought he might see Absolum among the prisoners.

On his return from America, degree in hand, Absolum had been sent to work at the Museum of National Culture where Benjamin was the recently appointed Director of Exhibits. There were, in fact, precious few exhibits but Absolum had tackled his new job with a will, doing his best to expand Benjamin's department. The young man's enthusiasm was infectious. In the few months Absolum was at the Museum, Benjamin came to regard his own posting there as less the political exile it was and more a job worth doing in itself.

Of course what Absolum did not know, and somehow led Benjamin into forgetting, was that in Karamoja doing a job too well was far more dangerous that doing it too poorly. The finger puppets, a very ancient and traditional form of entertainment from the Lake Province, drew attention. One morning plain-clothes officers from the State Research Unit were waiting on the Museum steps. Absolum disappeared and a few days later Benjamin was sacked.

So, each year Benjamin went to watch the prisoners but Absolum was never among them. Yesterday he had, for the first time, even approached one of the warders leaning on his old Lee Enfield rifle. But the warder had never heard of Absolum and impatiently waved Benjamin away before he could question any of the other guards.

Turning off Zambezi Benjamin had made his way down a steep muddy street into a quarter known as the Reservoir. The unpaved road once led traffic into the main thoroughfare above, but the rains of season after season had washed away the surface leaving holes and crevices too deep for any vehicle to negotiate. At some point, the road having been given up for lost, a huge garbage bin had been parked in its center and then forgotten. Animated by the hum of flies, trash and debris spilled out of it and onto the broken sidewalk.

On the shady side of the bin, under an overhang of garbage, a girl child of about three squatted to shit. She waved a piece of maize stalk to keep an emaciated pie dog at bay. Finished, she scraped her ass with the stalk and toddled off as the hungry dog slunk forward to eat.

Benjamin had picked his way through trash to the end of the street and entered the Speke Grill. He sat at a table and bought a copy of the Daily Salvation Messenger. The news vendor was a man of about forty with one leg and horrifying facial scars. The victim of a grenade blast during one of the endless wars for Karamojan freedom . . . or unity, or justice, or whatever they had been fought for. Without being asked, the Grill proprietor had set a cup of tea in front of Benjamin.

The newspaper had several long and laudatory pieces tracing the heroic, wise and compassionate career of The Wise One. A commentary explained why political parties and elections were unnecessary in Karamoja and discussed in great detail the love and adulation with which "99.9% of the population" regarded the MNS chairman.

On his way home Benjamin had studied posters, bearing the benevolent likeness of the nation's Husband and Father, which were plastered in great profusion over the corrugated tin walls of the Reservoir hovels. Most of those posters had been torn or turned into crude caricatures. The unreformed one-tenth of one per cent were apparently a maliciously active lot.

The Salvation Messenger had also reported that, during his Independence day message to the nation, His Excellency would announce introduction of a new 10,000 Karam note. Reliable and highly placed sources who, nevertheless, "did not wish to be named," also told the Messenger this new currency would bear the Great Leader's portrait. In tortured and convoluted phrases it was further indicated that the monetary appearance of the Presidential Likeness would put an end to inflation and repeated devaluations.

Benjamin had re-read the article carefully but could not discover the precise connection between the National Saviour's smile and a stable currency.

Benjamin was called back to the present by a group of MNS youth wingers marching along Acacia below his window. They were beating drums and singing and carried a large banner proclaiming the duty of all citizens to demonstrate their solidarity with the anti-imperialist struggle by attending that day's rally in the Square of the Unknown Martyr. There was a tone of hysteria in their shouting.

Benjamin turned from the window. For today, he would forgo his newspaper and tea at the Speke Grill. He switched the radio on again but the same announcer was now discussing the economic benefits which were to flow from recent barter trade agreements signed by the First Depositor of the Karamoja Development Bank with Libya and Rumania. Benjamin turned it off with an impatient snap.

On the bookshelf sat a photo of his infant granddaughter in Canada. The picture was six...no seven...years old now, so the little girl he had never seen in the flesh was no longer a baby but already at school. He tried to imagine what her life in that foreign country, where it was so cold, must be like. He wondered if she would be the only black child in her class. He tried to picture what sort of house she might live in. A knock at his door brought him back to Karamoja with a start.

In the unlit hallway Benjamin found Maria smiling in her shy way. She was dressed in her starched and freshly pressed school uniform. In her hand she held a Karamoja flag stapled to a piece of split bamboo.

"My dear. You've not gone to the square yet? You'll be late."
Benjamin was smiling widely. It always cheered him when Maria
called.

Maria looked serious, and in a voice too mature for her twelve
years said, "Those who go too early must stand in front against the
ropes. Then, later, when the crowd pushes forward they are the
ones to be beaten by the policemen's sticks. It is better to go later."

Benjamin's smile faded a little. "Yes, I see your point."

"May I come in?"

"Oh, indeed. Of course." Benjamin shuffled out of the narrow
doorway. "I have a fresh packet of biscuits. The ones you like so
much. I found a shop with just this one package left." He busied
himself at the table opening the cellophane wrapper and placing a
half dozen biscuits on a chipped plate.

Maria was Benjamin's niece. The daughter of his youngest sister and her husband Zachary. Benjamin had not laid eyes on his
sister or brother-in-law since Zachary had been appointed Under
Secretary for Political Affairs in the Movement of National Salvation five years before. Maria had been forbidden to visit him as
well, though she did so at least once each week.

Benjamin noticed that today Maria carried no bag. It was her
habit, on each visit, to bring him a gift, something "pinched" as
she put it, from her family's well stocked larder. Usually it was a
tin of meat, a jar of tomato sauce or even a bottle of gin. Maria had
begun this habit shortly after hearing her father comment that he
was now "feeding his family at the trough of power." When she repeated the story to Benjamin he could see that, young as she was,
Maria had been offended. Whether her stolen gifts were merely
charity to the uncle now banished from that trough or an attempt
to spite her father, he did not know. In any case, there was no sack
today, so he would be spared the humiliation of Maria's gift at
least for this week.

"You will not go to the Martyr's Square?" she asked.

"No."

"I didn't suppose you would," she said, accepting a biscuit from
the plate. "Have you ever gone?"

"I went one year."

Maria sat on a stool beside Benjamin's chair. "Yes, once is quite enough, isn't it?"

The crisp, almost adult tone and direction of Maria's conversation unsettled him, as it often did. It reminded him too much of the bush armies where children also learned to speak, and act, like adults long before their time.

Maria took another biscuit from the plate. "I think I'll just stay here with you."

"You really should be there, Maria," Benjamin protested. "Your class prefect, or even your teacher, may note your absence."

She laughed at that. "No Uncle, I will not be missed."

Benjamin sighed and took a biscuit for himself.

"Show me the puppets," Maria said.

Benjamin laughed, "It is some time since you've wanted to see the puppets."

"Show me," she asked again.

Benjamin pushed himself out of his chair and went to the sideboard. From a high shelf he took down a wooden box of the type which might contain chess pieces. He laid it on the table and opened it.

Maria sat on a chair and leaned forward to watch. Intricately carved from wood, each puppet was about six inches high and fitted with loops of string on the back through which Benjamin fitted his fingers.

Humming a tune from his childhood he moved his fingers so the puppets bounced, dancing in step.

Over the tin roof tops they could hear the band of the Presidential Guard lead the anniversary parade down Nile Street and into Zambezi, escorting the Great Leader to the Square of the Unknown Martyr. Benjamin stopped humming. The rhythm of the puppets shifted slightly until they marched across the tabletop toward Maria in step with the army band.

"You pinched the puppets from the Museum, didn't you Uncle?"

Benjamin turned and gazed out the window in silence, but the puppets continued to march.

"Last night, I heard Father talking to Mama. He said you would have been sent to prison had the puppets been found . . . but that you hid them."

Benjamin closed his eyes. The puppets marched on and on. Maria was silent for a time, then in a much softer voice she went on. "Father said another man was shot because he would not tell where the puppets had gone."

Benjamin opened his eyes. "Absolum was shot!?"

Maria shrugged. "Was that his name? Someone was shot. Why?"

Benjamin had no answer. Why had so many been shot? Killed in bush wars and prison yards? Why had so many more died in reprisals and of the disease and hunger left in their wake? He looked down at the tramping puppets. The band outside had reached the square now and the music came to a crashing halt. The puppets stopped marching.

"Were you not afraid I would tell someone about the puppets?" she asked.

"Sometimes," he admitted. "But your visits have always been our secret, haven't they?"

"Yes. Though Mama may suspect."

Benjamin nodded.

"But the reason I could never speak of the puppets was different." Maria reached out and touched a figure on Benjamin's left hand. "This one, you see, looks like Father. And this one," she touched the puppet on Benjamin's index finger, "looks like President Andanha."

Benjamin studied the child. "And that frightened you?"

"A little," Maria nodded, "but I was more frightened by the way they have different faces, but still all dance in time."

Benjamin nodded again. "Yes . . . that frightens me as well," he murmured.

Bouquet

IT WAS DARK and he wanted light, but the bulb was broken.

The kerosine lantern was there, but his trembling hands would never manage the job of lifting the globe and striking a match and putting it to the wick. The last of the fuel had been burned up in any case, though he did not remember that.

He lay watching the lantern skate figures through the dust and clutter on the bedside table, troubling himself about being unable to make a light.

A light and the lantern seemed very important and he studied the metal and glass curves for a long time before it occurred to him that if he could see the lantern then it must be day and he had no need to strike a match.

He laughed. A self-mocking, hysterical, choking sound. What was required was to open the shutter. Perhaps that could be managed.

He straightened his legs. He lifted an arm. He moved. His body hit the floor, face down, with a wet thud like bread dough slapped into a pan.

He laughed again and tasted blood in his mouth.

His face lay in something wet and sticky and the stench of old vomit gagged him. Laughter turned to retching.

He heaved, and heaved again, sending knives of burning pain through his body, but there was nothing to throw up. He was lying in the remains of his last meal, a half tin of grease-congealed Romanian corned beef, eaten sometime the day before and, in his suffering, puked onto the floor.

He managed to roll onto his back, putting a little distance between himself and the rancid puke.

The pointless retching stopped. He rested for a time, waiting for the pain to subside, then turned onto his belly again and lifted himself to his hands and knees.

René stared at him from the shadows, cloudy eyes expressing surprise and incomprehension and accusation.

"Fuck you, you bastard!" he rasped. The words were nearly inaudible, drowned in the gurgle of blood in his own throat. René stared back in silence.

The window was behind him. Crawling like a baby, disoriented, head hanging loose, he made a slow circle and crossed the meter and a half of packed earth floor. He turned and sat, his back to the wall, gathering such strength as remained. The plastered mud was cool against his bare shoulders. It felt good and comforting.

He wondered what dying men were supposed to think about. Perhaps eternity and making peace with their gods. He leaned his head against the wall. As he had his whole life he decided to avoid the present by pretending, however briefly, that it did not exist. That it would go away.

Yet a diminishing part of him knew it would not. He knew that this time it was he who would go away, but it is hard to change the habits of a lifetime. If thirty-six years could be called a lifetime.

He coughed, and again tasted blood.

He would think of something better, but it would be easier to do so in the light.

He reached above him. The window was low and by stretching just a little he could grasp the burglar bars. With a groaning effort he pulled himself up and around.

He swayed, leaning against the wall, both arms hooked through the bars, clinging to them as the world tilted and spun out of control. He hung on, gritting his teeth. If he let the bars swirl away now he would never have the strength to catch them again. The window would remain closed and he would die in the dark.

After a hurtling, time-warped voyage through outer and inner space, the ride slowed and the earth steadied.

He opened his eyes and watched fingers fumble with the bolt.

The strange stubby objects stabbing at the catch seemed to have little to do with him. When it slid free he banged his forehead against the rough planks and the shutter swung away.

Instinct, over-riding his weakness, raised his hands to protect pain-stabbed eyes from the glare of day and he fell. His face scraped down the cracked and pitted wall.

He would not die in the dark.

He would die, and he would die soon. Death would come before night defeated his open shutter and took away the light. But he would not die in the dark.

The thought pleased him very much. He smiled, happy with his small victory.

The light brought other rewards. Beside him, within reach of where he lay beneath the window, was a chair. A bottle of water and a glass stood on the seat. Under it was a half bottle of country gin.

He smiled again, and spoke. "There is a god."

A cigarette would have been good too and, somewhere in the room, if he could find his shirt, there were cigarettes. But he couldn't smoke anymore, he knew that. He needed no doctor to tell him the jagged metal had lodged in his lung.

Very slowly he pulled air into his chest, breathing as deeply as pain would allow. Hoisting himself into a sitting position again, he sat beside the chair, back to the wall facing the door and René.

It occurred to him that this would be a good way for her to find him, but quickly banished the macabre image. He must pretend none of this was happening, that it would go away.

But it was she who had gone away. She had gone somewhere. He tried very hard to remember where and why, but he could not. She had said she was coming back, but you could never trust a whore, and when she came he knew it would already be too late.

All that was certain was that she was not with René.

In an instant he was crushed by grief and self-pity. The bitch had gone away. She had left him to die alone.

Tears welled up in his eyes and cut crooked tracks through the dirt on his face.

With great care he took the bottle and glass from the chair. He half-filled the glass with gin and cut it with water. He sipped.

The liquor burned into his raw throat and his stomach contracted.

He sighed, settling against the wall. Holy Joseph. In the south, in her country, they called their home-made gin Holy Joseph. He did not know why and, though he had always wondered, he had never asked. Surely the answer to that question, at least, would have been harmless. He wished she would come in time so that he might yet ask why it was called Holy Joseph.

He wished she would come.

He stared at the floor, at the tiny oblong patch of light cast by the sun entering the window. He watched dust devils dance. He listened to children playing somewhere in a compound nearby.

Images came back as from some story he had read a long long time ago, or a half-forgotten movie he had seen, or perhaps only heard about.

A life lived in the third person.

He thought of other places and other times. Earlier times. Times that could have been yesterday or before God said "Let there be light." Good times and bad times. Even first times.

* * *

He stared into his drink. He was waiting for the unidentified object suspended within the ice cube to be freed at last from its frozen cell.

He wasn't very much worried about swallowing it, whatever it was, when it finally floated free. Mostly he was just curious to know what it might be and to speculate upon how it might have come to be there.

He poked at the ice cube with his finger, slopping some of the whiskey and coke onto the bar. Whatever it was, it seemed to have legs, but he couldn't be sure.

The boy washing glasses at a small sink in front of him wrung his cloth, lifted the glass, and wiped up the spill, taking the opportunity to peep into the drink, curious about what the white man found so absorbing.

The waiter made a sympathetic clicking noise with his tongue. "Sorry, Patron. Ice block no be clean." He reached for a spoon and began to fish in Durelle's glass for the offending ice cube.

"No! No, leave it!" Durelle protested, pulling the glass from the boy's grasp, slopping another spill onto the counter top in the process. "It's almost free. You can't spoil it now. I've been waiting too long."

The boy stared for a moment, obviously puzzled, but being offered no further explanation he shrugged, wiped the bar a second time, and went back to his sink. This customer was not truly drunk, not yet anyway, but then white men, drunk or sober, were such curious, unpredictable creatures their behaviour was best left unexplained.

Durelle prodded the ice cube once more and glanced down the bar.

There was a dice game set there. It was too far off to be seen clearly and he could not recall having noticed it before. It consisted of a large round board, felt-covered and enclosed by a thick padded rail. There were at least six and perhaps eight chunky white dice. Games in general interested him very little but he was in a speculative frame of mind and wondered what it might be.

A woman stood there, one of those women in whom the girl would always be seen. Tall and graceful and arrestingly beautiful, she tossed the dice over and over again into the felt-lined pit. He decided this rolling of the dice was symbolic, perhaps even intentionally so on her part. Symbolic of just what he wasn't sure, but something about the rolling of the dice spoke of ritual and symbolism.

He had not seen her come in. She must have arrived when he was distracted by the frozen mystery of his drink, or while the waiter was attempting to steal what he had paid good money for.

Leaning on his forearms over the glass he examined the ice once more. Whatever was lodged there had come no closer to liberty. He imagined he was watching himself trapped within the cold and hostile cube. "Too much symbolism around here tonight," he mumbled.

"Patron?" the boy responded, looking up from his sink.

He looked at the boy, realizing he had spoken aloud. "Symbolism," he shrugged. "A sort of philosophical ju-ju by which we explain and evaluate our troubled souls . . . like that piece of shit stuck in my ice cube here . . . " He pointed deep into his glass.

The boy shook his head. "No be shit, Patron. No be ju-ju. A fly I think." The waiter looked very serious and once again picked up his spoon.

"Oh no you don't," he growled, grabbing his glass and holding it away at arm's length. "That's my ju-ju in there. I paid for it and you're not to fuck with it!"

This time the boy did not go back to work at the sink, he walked to the opposite end of the bar, near the dice game. It was apparent he wanted to put as much distance as possible between himself and the crazy white man with the dirty ice cube.

She was still there, rolling dice.

Beside the game board her drink stood untouched. She swept up, threw the dice, swept them up and tossed them again in one long, fluid, repetitive motion. She barely glanced at the numbers turning up, often rolling the ivory cubes back into her hand even before they had come fully to rest. Once in every three or four rolls her eyes swept the crowd along the bar, though her hand went right on shooting the dice. Then, attracted perhaps by his stare, her gaze rested upon him for a moment, but the rhythm of the dice continued uninterrupted. She smiled.

He returned her smile across the distance and nodded in what he hoped was a noncommittal way.

With some difficulty he turned his attention back to his ice cube. Not much progress. He spun it over with another jab of his finger. From one side it seemed to have legs all right, from the other it seemed not.

"You've been living here for some time haven't you?" She was beside him, sitting on a stool he had thought occupied by a fat sweaty German.

He looked up. "I don't really live here, I just drink a lot and do most of it here. I have a house."

She laughed at that. "Yes, I'm sure you do, and a family as well," she said flicking his wedding band with her finger. "I meant you've been living in Africa for some time."

"Why do you say that?" It was his habit to give away as little as possible, to avoid answering questions whenever it could be politely managed or to give answers open to interpretation. He was not secretive, he had just come to regard all questions as fundamentally unanswerable, even the simple ones. How long was "some time?"

"I can always tell the 'Johnnies Just Come' from the 'Blackfeet.'"

"And what makes you think I'm not a JJC?"

She smiled, her eyes twinkling in a way which accused him of evasion. "Your shirt sleeves. I can always tell how long a white man has been here by the way he rolls his shirt sleeves."

He laughed and looked at the sleeves of his bush shirt rolled about midway between wrist and elbow. "So how long have I been here?"

She shrugged, still smiling. "Its not a very exact science, but for some time. I'd say about ten years."

"Closer to fifteen," he admitted, his voice trailing away.

She laid her cigarette in the ash tray and pulled his arm toward her. "About time for another turn of the sleeve don't you think?" Her fingers were warm and soft against his bare forearm.

As she folded his sleeve she paid no attention to what her hands were doing but fixed her wide-eyed gaze directly on his face. Her eyes drew him. The blend of red and blue light from above the bar softened them and washed their darkness with an icy blue luminance . . . or so it seemed.

"Do you have a name?" he asked.

"I am called Bouquet."

"I can see why," he told her with a mock sigh.

She smiled at that. "My christening name is Bouquellen, but I am called Bouquet. And you? Do you have a name?"

"Not one that matters."

She touched his arm again. "That cannot be true. A name can matter very much."

He looked up again, into the ice-blue eyes. "I am Durelle," he said.

* * *

He shifted to a more comfortable position and took another careful sip of Holy Joseph. A cockroach, disturbed by the light, launched itself from atop the door frame and ended a long de-

scending flight across the room by striking him squarely in the left
eye.

The roach crashed to the floor beside him and he watched it, injured and buzzing on its back, struggling to right itself and escape
to the dark safety of a corner or a crack in the wall. It did not want
to die in the light.

He looked up at the ceiling. The ju-ju charm was unharmed. It
hung from its string, knotted to a rusted nail. It was simply a small
envelope of paper, perhaps five centimeters square, wrapped in
black and white thread and what it contained he could not guess.
He had discovered similar charms attached to each of her bed
posts and tucked beneath the mattress corners but had never
dared open one. He had asked about them once, but received no
real answer.

* * *

"What's the ju-ju for? You trying to keep something away or
bait something into your net?"

"It is to help me sleep."

"You have trouble sleeping?"

"Not anymore."

"Did you bring it with you from the village?"

"My father prepared it."

"Your father is a bush doctor?"

"Are you afraid of a little bush medicine white man?"

He told her he was not afraid of ju-ju charms, and that day he
was telling the truth. In time he became less certain. She possessed
a strange and mighty power. He could not conceive of it originating in the ju-ju charm, but who could be sure and, whatever its
source, it was just as mysterious. Pass too close to Bouquet and
you were pulled and anchored into her field of gravity. One became a satellite moon, locked forever in a trajectory dictated by
Bouquet and Bouquet alone.

By the time he had even thought to ask about the charm he had,
already, somehow joined a constellation of human planets named
Juliette and Bridgitte and Michel and Vanessa and Fouda... and
the hidden moon, René.

All of them orbited Bouquet, the center of a unique universe of captured spirits, a tiny planetary system turning on orbital paths within the poto poto walls and beneath the leaking roof of a shabby house like ten thousand others in the quarter . . . except, in this one, burned a sun called Bouquet.

Pulled in, Durelle found a female world. A world smelling of hair oil, of perfume and of something forever cooking on the stove. It was a world which sounded of women's voices, in shouts or laughter or tears. It was a world in which tables, chairs, shelves and doorframes were littered with colourful skirts and silk blouses and skimpy underwear. Shoes lined the walls and jewelry appeared in coffee cups.

As accommodation in the quarter went, it was a large house. Five rooms tacked together, one added to the other, then expanded or improved upon as small funds became available. When it rained, the roof leaked and muddy streams swept a stew of rotten garbage, garnished with beads of goat and chicken shit, past the door sill and slopping onto the kitchen floor if the storm was a heavy one.

Excepting the number of rooms, the house was like thousands of others surrounding it, packed so close, wall to wall, eave to eave, that window shutters opened only part way and the late night rattle of a chamber pot would awaken neighbours on four sides. Inside, though, this house boasted luxuries unknown to most of its neighbours.

The largest room served, at the end closest to the door, as kitchen. There was a tall electric refrigerator and a full-sized gas stove . . . not just the common tabletop cooker but the model with an oven. There were the usual stew pots cast of recycled aluminum but there were also enamelled and stainless steel utensils and, like a ghost from that world Durelle only wished to escape, a teflon frying pan.

He found the heavy-duty blender, in which huge batches of volcanic pepper sauce were prepared on an almost daily basis, even more bizarre. As the realization grew that, in Bouquet's life, the past was present and time could stand still, her kitchen came to haunt and accuse him. The refrigerator mocked him, humming "interloper, interloper" each time he passed and the blender screamed insults about "poor whites" each time it was given voice. Even before he heard the name, and long before he saw the face, René was there.

At the other extremity of the frontroom was the salon, less troubling in that it contained little more than a locally made couch with three matching chairs set around a low table which could never be made to sit solidly on the cracked concrete floor. But on the shelf under that table, buried beneath a pile of ancient magazines, was the photo album and, when brought out of hiding, that album had destroyed him.

The house and its furnishings, after a third whiskey as the light of day failed, or on a misty rainy afternoon, sent him hostile messages and hints of hidden mysteries he could never interpret. Still, it was only mud and concrete and wood and tin and it was a home, of sorts. It sheltered people. People who, like himself, not knowing where they belonged, or having somehow slipped from where they may have belonged, came to live in a state of servitude and bondage to Bouquet.

Even as he slowly bled to death propped against the wall of her bedroom Durelle still puzzled over her power. Whether it came from her father's medicine charm nailed to the ceiling, or was simply born within her, he would now never know, but the power manifested itself in, and was exercised through, the greatest ju-ju of all . . . money.

If he had reached any conclusions at all, it was that Bouquet was one of those rare people who somehow understood money and how to direct and control its power.

Juliette slept in a room off the kitchen. Technically Bouquet's aunt, in as much as she was Bouquet's mother's sister, she was in fact two years younger than Bouquet. She was a big rangy woman with broad flat features beneath back-combed hair which she vainly and mistakenly believed made her look like Tina Turner. She was not beautiful, nor even pretty in the usual sense, but she was handsome and had her own magnetism and, to Durelle, the best legs in the house.

Others must have shared his opinion of those legs, and more, because Juliette seemed forever pregnant, or at least late with her period, or perhaps just incapable of counting the days of the month. Just as often she caught the clap.

Juliette ventured forth each evening and plied her trade with more success, perhaps, than she could deal with. She had an instinct for men and their weaknesses which outstripped her more physically attractive competition. She ingratiated herself with bar and night club owners and never paid a cover charge. In even the most difficult circumstances she avoided the attention of the police. Still, she was incapable of taking precautions against conception or infection and once a month ran to Bouquet in tears with one or the other and, on occasion, both.

Bouquet would know what to do. She knew which antispasmodic drugs induced miscarriage in the early weeks. If it was too late, she knew which doctor could be relied upon for a reasonably painless, reasonably sanitary, and reasonably priced abortion. If the problem was *pisse-chaude* she knew which antibiotics to buy and the dosages to use.

Durelle had quickly developed a real affection for Juliette. She was cheerful and kind towards him and, he had to admit, mothered him a little. But at any time Bouquet and he were together in the same room Juliette disappeared. In the worst of times he would think of seeking Juliette's intercession with Bouquet but he knew she would never agree. She was totally dependent upon Bouquet and, moreover, he could see in her eyes she feared her as well.

Bouquet manipulated Juliette with her fear, with her guilt, and stupidity . . . and with a dream.

In their village, further south, Bouquet was building. The concrete walls and sheet metal roof of what would one day be a shop and bar, with an apartment behind, had already been completed. The floors were not yet poured, nor the doors and windows installed, and daily contributions toward continuation of the project were extorted through the simple promise of allowing Juliette to serve in the bar when the job was done.

Each morning Bouquet collected, offering no accounting in return and no participation in the undertaking beyond employment as a bar maid.

"The least you could do is offer a few share certificates in 'Bouquellen Enterprises,'" Durelle sighed, knowing full well he was venturing into dangerous territory.

Bouquet laughed at that. "She can't even remember to take her pill. She's never learned to count the safe days. How would she ever manage to put up a real building without letting the contractors rob her . . . or, when the building is done, make a profit from a bar or shop?"

Durelle knew she was right, but the sense of injustice lingered. "Just the same, she's got a lot of money tied up in your property . . . money earned by the sweat of her ass . . . it just seems . . . "

"This is family, Durelle," she snapped, cutting him off. "Stay out of it! This is not your affair."

Once again he knew she was right. At the same time he knew she was wrong. Bouquet was always right and wrong simultaneously.

Bridgitte was Bouquet's sister but, like all relationships in this cluster of human asteroids, even that connection was incomplete. They were half-sisters, children of a mutual father by different mothers.

Bridgitte was short and round and physically the least blessed of the three women. Through Bouquet's guidance with makeup and hairstyling and Juliette's advice on dressing and living on the downtown streets, she survived.

Everything beyond their own tiny universe Bridgitte treated as a joke. Even when Durelle felt as though everything had been lost, she could make him laugh aloud with her constant, rapid-fire repertoire of stories, one-liners and comic commentary delivered in a broken mixture of Ewondo, French and Pidgin . . . though he had to admit her machine gun speech prevented him from understanding even half of what she said.

But Bouquet and Juliette were never a joke. If there was jealousy in Bridgitte's heart it was buried deep, but the sense of envy was palatable when she watched them dress for the evening.

So many times Durelle had wanted to shout, "You stupid girl, there is nothing here to envy," but he could never say it, in those words or others, because without the hope of succeeding at the game as had Juliette and Bouquet, she could imagine nothing else at all.

Bouquet had the beauty and style, and Juliette had the magnetism and street smarts. They had been entrusted with the secret powers demanded by a life beneath the whirling lights of chrome and velvet-lined nightclubs on the mountainside. Bridgitte was left to prowl cafes and cheap bars on the side streets.

Bouquet had, without apparent effort or perhaps even much enthusiasm, snared a white man and when he had inevitably "gone back" she repeated the miracle. Bridgitte navigated the murky world of minor government clerks, small-time traders and taxi-drivers. Juliette, though she had yet to make one her own, at least knew many white men and a professor or two from the university, and even a diplomat from the Senegalese embassy.

Still, in Bridgitte, the sense of humour seemed to feed the spirit (or perhaps it was the other way round) and, cheerfully enough, she went off each evening to a world where the lights were yellow to discourage insect swarms and where the beer was always warm. While the reality did little to daunt Bridgitte's spirit, imagining it could depress and sometimes anger Durelle. Especially when, in 500-franc coins, Bridgitte too handed over her contribution to the building fund.

"You're a goddamn pimp," he growled at Bouquet.

She just clicked her tongue.

"Shit! You're on both sides of the fence. You're a whore and a pimp!"

She dropped the lid onto a cooking pot with a jarring crash and turned to face him where he lay on the couch picking the label from a whiskey bottle with his thumb nail. "And what does that make you Durelle?" She was laughing, but not with amusement. "The pimps and whores pay the rent here."

He was already regretting his comment and the opening of a subject best left closed, but he was also angry and a little drunk. "I make my contribution," he mumbled defensively.

She tucked her kaba between her legs and squatted at the spice stone, laughing again. "We won't be holidaying in Paris this year on your contribution."

"You send your own sister out to fuck pousse pousse boys and taxi men. It's not right."

The fist-sized grinding stone crashed into the table beside him smashing a beer bottle and showering him in a hail of broken glass.

"You self-righteous bastard!" she screamed. "You abandon your wife and a whole life ten thousand people in this quarter can only dream of to come down here and slum with whores and pimps for the sake of the Great West African Novel. You fuck me and then sit in my bedroom pretending to write and you still have the balls to set yourself above me and my sister and pousse pousse boys? Christ! Who do you think you are? We may not be making much of a success of our lives, but we haven't failed yet either. You screwed up in your own world and you offer nothing to ours!"

He picked a shard of glass from his beard. "I don't buy refrigerators and teflon frying pans . . . and I can't afford to put the floor in that enterprise of yours . . . if that's what you mean."

"Listen to me, you piece of drunken white shit," she hissed, "I could make enough in one week at the Hotel Grande to buy three refrigerators . . ."

"So what are you doing here scraping away at your grinding stone?"

She froze for a moment, then turned and ran outside, but he saw no tears. She was gone for a long time, but when she came back they drank the rest of the whiskey and spent the remaining hours till dawn in sweaty, noisy sex.

The young man behind the third ill-fitting door personified, to Durelle, the absolute and utter tyranny Bouquet exercised upon them all.

Fouda, though a son and the issue of their father's senior wife, had, it seemed, been sent as a sacrificial lamb to this unnatural worship of the daughter Bouquet. It was his duty to represent the whole family's constant and unending devotion. It was Fouda's role to stand and serve.

He was an offering furnished to the power of the goddess Bouquet, and Bouquet, as she accepted the devotion of them all, received the offering as her due and as her right and she used Fouda as it was meant that he should be used.

Bouquet was the next to youngest of her father's five children. She was the only child of her mother, her mother was the junior of her father's two wives and, above all, she was a woman child. Yet even her family, far off in the village, deferred to her. Her advice was sought, and acted upon for even the most trivial matters, and her smallest whim was fulfilled as if a command. On behalf of those absent, Fouda served.

He served without objection or complaint and Durelle watched and puzzled. The male child of the senior wife, serving at the beck and call of the only daughter of a junior wife? It defied understanding, it defied tradition and it defied logic.

Durelle felt he was living at the center of an African Cinderella story with a big, strapping, eighteen-year old village boy playing the role of Cinderella while, in Bouquet, the ugly step sister had become a beautiful half sister.

Though never explained, Durelle gathered that, at Bouquet's expense, Fouda had learned the mysteries of the automobile at a local trade school. Eventually the boy found a few days' employment each week as an apprentice mechanic at a garage near the taxi park.

If this placed Fouda under obligation, it appeared the garage owner also owed some money to Bouquet and engaged Fouda's assistance when extra hands were needed and perhaps just as often when they were not. Such small amounts as Fouda earned in this way were paid by his employer directly to Bouquet. He would come, late in the evening, and personally deliver the money to Bouquet.

Directly, Fouda received not a franc. He would sit in the salon wearing a tight smile and watch his pay day executed by proxy at the door. When his employer was gone he might, very rarely, ask if he could have some small sum with which to see a movie or buy a beer with his friends. Even more rarely Bouquet would hand over a few francs, which Fouda accepted as a supplicant with both hands cupped at arm's length before him. More often his sister simply ignored the request, pretending not even to have heard. Fouda would never ask a second time.

On many of those occasions, when his tattered pockets were left empty, he would, if Bouquet left the room or turned her back, beg Durelle for the price of a beer or a movie ticket. If he had it himself, Durelle, more often than not, slipped Fouda a thousand-franc note.

Bouquet must have known or at least guessed that he was giving Fouda the money she refused him, but nothing was ever said about that. If, though, he ever poured Fouda a shot of whiskey it brought a landslide of Ewondo invective upon both their heads.

"We're going to have one drink for God's sake!" Durelle protested.

"He's too young."

"He's eighteen years old."

"He's my brother, not yours. I decide what is too young."

Drunk one night, Durelle had fought back. "He's only your half brother, and full or half you don't own him! You don't own any of us!"

She grabbed the glass away from Fouda and swept the whiskey bottle from the table, taking both to her room.

"It's my whiskey, you bitch! I paid for it!" he yelled after her.

She came and stood in the doorway glaring at them. "It's not who owns what or who," she snapped, "but everything entering this house . . . you and Fouda and your whiskey . . . stays or goes at my pleasure. This is my house!"

"Nobody owns a whore house," he screamed back, "it's public property!"

Her door slammed with such force he could hear the wood splinter. Fouda sat staring straight ahead, saying nothing and wearing the same tight grin he affected when his salary was paid to Bouquet. Durelle tried to persuade Fouda to come with him to a bar where they could drink all the whiskey they wanted, but Fouda refused. The dinner dishes had not been washed, he said. Durelle went and drank alone.

So it went on. Fouda cleaned, a dozen times a day he ran

errands to the market, he washed the laundry and pressed the clothes. Durelle would lie on the bed watching Bouquet dress and shake his head in wonder when, having selected her blouse and skirt and underwear, she would shout for Fouda and hurl the chosen wardrobe through the curtains into the salon where Fouda seemed forever waiting, his iron already hot.

He had continued slipping Fouda such change as he could afford and, when Bouquet was out or not watching, even managed to share with him an occasional shot of whiskey. In their own way he and Fouda attempted an unspoken alliance to counter Bouquet's tyranny over them, but it was an ineffective treaty and one which checked Bouquet's power not at all.

The path to Bouquet's house was narrow. It wound up a slope from a cracked and broken street, between low houses squatting shoulder to shoulder. In the rain it was slick and treacherous with mud.

The little track was at its steepest and most difficult just where it approached her door. An out-of-use stand pipe, bent and crooked, leaned there, sealed off, but leaking a steady stream of water into the mud. Even in the dry season the footing near the pipe would have been impossible were it not for the square cement slab imbedded in the slope. Durelle had crossed it many times before, one afternoon, when the light fell at just the right angle, he noticed the slab was crudely engraved. A grave stone.

The letters had been worn thin by the constant trickle of water from the leaky pipe and the scuffing of a million gritty feet. The surname was gone, except for a crooked capital A and what might have been an R. The Christian name was more complete and could have been Albert, but he was not sure. The date of birth, if ever recorded, had completely disappeared, but 1937 was clearly etched as the date of death. Below the faded lettering was the sign of the cross.

"Who's buried out front?" he had asked.

Bouquet just shrugged.

The gravestone, too, became significant . . . as everything began slowly to fall apart, to come unstuck, to crumble into little rotten pieces.

Each time he stepped over it, it felt like crossing to the other side of existence. It became the gate post to his own personal hell. It even occurred to him that all his suffering was a curse levied by the ghost of that man without a name who had lain dead for fifty years with muddy feet stamping over his tomb. Perhaps a half century of such disrespect had finally brought on retribution and Durelle had just been unfortunate enough to come to the wrong place at the wrong time.

On one of the bad days, on one of those hot, humid, rain and whiskey-soaked afternoons when he was sure she was killing him, he had brought it up again. "Who's buried at the doorstep? One of your old lovers?"

"Don't be ridiculous."

"Did he die easier than me? I die hard, don't I? The damned always die hard."

She just made a hissing sound and rattled the magazine she was pretending to read.

"Do you suppose there's room to put me there too?"

"Maybe that's only a stone," she snapped, but something in her tone told him he had gotten to her, just a little. She was superstitious, in her way, and perhaps she was a little more uncomfortable with stepping, day after day, on a tombstone than she cared to admit. "If it is a grave," she added, "it was there twenty five years before I was born."

"So your birth certificate says," he laughed bitterly, "but you've been around since the beginning of time and you'll ride with the horsemen of the apocalypse." He went and stood at the door, under the dripping eve, and watched rivulets of blood-red water snake down the path and across the gravestone.

"You're drunk," she said.

"Not drunk enough," he told the rain and he wondered, for the first time, how he might kill René.

* * *

In shadows above the door where light from the tiny window could not reach, he saw her riding tandem behind the second horseman, galloping through the final smoke and fire.

Wild and primitive and naked, breasts flattened against the horseman's back, her coal black skin shone with a glow deeper even than when she came, rubbed slick with oil, from her bath. The muscles of her thighs rippled strong and firm where her legs gripped the animal's blood-red flanks. The ropey strength of her back stood out in dark relief as spears of lightning stabbed through smoky clouds above her.

The horseman's sword flashed back the glow of flames and his eyes were burning embers as he rose in the stirrups and turned toward her. Her braids streamed behind on super-heated wind and she leaned forward shouting something Durelle could not hear. Words of encouragement for the horseman, or words of direction, or hate . . . perhaps even words of love.

The four riders, each in his way, were ugly and twisted and horrible as they lunged from the gates of hell, the hooves of their horses clattering across a gravestone which bore only the sign of the cross and the date 1937. Yet, though her mouth and eyes were thrown wide in a shout of final victory, she was as beautiful and alluring as the night she stood silently shooting dice and searching for a victim among the faces at the bar.

She looked down, studying him where he slumped half naked and shivering against the wall of that fouled room, smelling of puke and blood, in a rotting house, built of mud on mud foundations, in the native quarter of a city which welcomed no one, least of all the interloper.

For just a moment, for a fleeting second, he thought he saw something else in those dark eyes which, to him, as always, somehow seemed blue. For just an instant did she betray some feeling, perhaps regret, or even pity . . . or was it, once again and still, just his fevered imagination letting him believe what he so much wanted to believe?

She was capable of loving. Perhaps she was never capable of loving him, perhaps it was as she said and she had never loved René, and perhaps, after the accident, she was capable of loving no one again, but there had been a time. She had loved Michel.

* * *

The news came at midday. The boy who was employed to escort children of the quarter to and from school, stood at the door breathless and wide-eyed with terror. There was blood on his shirt and on his hands. Durelle heard him speak not a word. He just stood there in a state of silent stony shock.

Those were still the good days. It now seemed this day, a Tuesday, was perhaps the last of the good days. Bouquet sat beside him on the sagging sofa, improving her English by reading aloud from a pornographic novel. They were laughing at a particularly outrageous description of oral sex when the boy came and stood, in speechless terror, at the door.

She looked at the boy and, very slowly, stood up. For a moment she seemed frozen there, turned to a block of ebony. Then, upsetting the coffee table and sending a chair spinning against the wall, she began to run.

He was close behind her as she went through the door, but even though it was nearly two kilometers to the scene, he never overtook her. She ran hard. She ran barefoot and silent. She ran directly down the center of the busy road with car and truck horns howling in protest. A dozen times he was certain she would be run down.

She reached the crumpled body with the last of her strength, stumbling and skidding and falling hard upon the asphalt beside it, sweeping the bloody torn remains of her six-year old son into trembling arms with a single scream of anguish. He knelt beside them, helpless.

The bush taxi stood nearby, smashed against the wall of a hairdressing salon. The bus had struck Michel from behind, dragging his fragile childish body, face down, over a hundred meters of pavement. To Durelle, the tiny corpse was so mangled as to be unidentifiable save for the blood-soaked remains of his clothing and the little St. Christopher medal, blessed, Bouquet had said, by the Pope himself, which René had sent his son from Rome.

The darkness had always been within her, lurking. Durelle had discovered it early. Controlled, it had been part of her allure. Michel was a charming, vibrant, wonderful little boy but, in truth, probably no more or less special than any little boy. Still, to a mother, to Bouquet, he was everything and a great deal more.

Durelle had not realized how much more until Michel was gone.

In the months that followed he began to sense that Michel had been life itself to Bouquet. As she was the sun centering his universe, it was Michel who had cast light into her life and kept the evil spirits of her soul hidden deep in shadow. Then, suddenly and without warning, on a hot sun-drenched afternoon, the light was extinguished and the devils slipped their chains.

Deep and lasting grief at the loss of a child, in itself, he could understand, but the soul-twisting bitterness which came to possess Bouquet was something more. Something much much deeper and more painful.

Until Michel's death they had lived each moment in a tumultuous present, rushing toward tomorrow, leaving yesterday to history. But cruel changes the accident wrought in Bouquet germinated in Durelle a new and destructive interest in the past. Bouquet's past.

She suffered for the loss of her child, but Michel was René's child as well. What else had she lost when the little boy was crushed beneath the wheels of the Mammie wagon?

The photograph, pasted into a dusty and dog-eared album, would have been easy to find had he ever gone looking. When, at last, he saw that picture it was not only René he found, but a grown Michel. A man of the future who would, now, never exist. If ever a son was the image of his father, Michel was. It was seeing the photograph which launched Durelle's own final descent into hell.

* * *

He was no longer strong enough to hold his head up unaided, but sitting as he was, he could rest it against the wall.

Slowly rolling his pain-stabbed skull from right to left, Durelle shifted until he could see the table where his papers lay, curled and mildewed. There were piles nearly a foot high, and others smaller and more scattered, but quantity had no relation to quality. Every word of it stunk.

He had tried to write of so many things. He had tried to write about all of them. About these women and men and children whirling in a dance marathon of survival. Especially he had tried to write about Michel and his death that afternoon and what it meant . . . what it meant to Bouquet and what it had come to represent to him . . . but he had always failed. He had failed because he understood nothing of what it all meant. He had no idea what anything meant to any of them. He sought self-exorcism through fiction, but story by story his fictional world replaced reality.

He had put a million words on paper, but succeeded in writing nothing because he understood nothing. He had never completed a story or a poem. He had, over and over, become bogged in the mire of trying to interpret meaning from the chaos his life had become. And René, in characters by a dozen different names, hunted and haunted him from paragraph to paragraph.

He now concluded that life had no significance or meaning whatever, that it was just as trivial and chaotic as it appeared, and that all the puzzles worth solving had no answers. Now he wondered what, through so many long hot days, could have driven his attempts to force all he saw and felt into files and categories and line items which so stubbornly refused to equal a balanced formula.

Over and over, denying the futility of it, he had tried to corral life's dilemma within fences built of words, and day after day the pieces escaped, stampeding away in a chaos of broken images. Words were smoke. . . .

As pencils wore down and the paper returned to pulp from the sweat of his hand, the enigma of René grew and Durelle's own hostility spread like a cancer on his soul.

As failure followed failure, and the pile of drafts grew taller and taller on his table, he had charged, heedless of consequence, into the cauldron of the city around him. He staggered into the muddy, potholed, half built backroads of a world to which he did not belong.

Out there it felt as though the essential clue he sought lay just around the corner, or glowed at the center of every street corner group. But as he approached, it would slip away, just a little further away. He stumbled into a world which greeted him with ambivalence, where he was neither welcome nor unwelcome. He had entered a world in which he did not exist. He did not exist because the inhabitants of that world simply regarded him as non-existent.

Even before he met Bouquet, the attempt had become an obsession. He was sucked deeper and deeper into the whirlpool, into a world complex and alive within itself but closed to him. At some point, and he could not even remember just when it might have been, he simply stopped going back to his own world.

It began as nights stretched later and later into the morning hours. Then one night he failed to return to his own world at all, to the air-conditioned house with the hot shower and the servants preparing breakfast and a wife who had long since written him off as a lunatic.

For a time he continued to work, but his office too became foreign territory, and soon he set it aside as well. He had never even gone back to learn at what point in his unexplained absence they had finally sacked him.

Having been cast, or having cast himself, adrift, he was easily drawn into Bouquet's tiny galaxy, adding a little more weight to that patched-together house as it slowly sank into the muddy hillside of the quarter.

His new life proved easy to sustain. Food and drink were cheap. With only a few francs a day, a man could eat in the tiny chophouses or at road side braziers, and stay permanently drunk in the off-licenses and bars. Earning those few francs took little effort.

For the first time in his life he made his living by his pen. He wrote letters for the illiterate citizens of his adopted world as they engaged in their endless struggle with a paper-choked government bureaucracy to obtain certificates of death, birth, marriage and employment, or official documents and authorizations of a thousand other kinds whose purpose he could never fathom.

At a reasonable fee he edited university term papers for grammar, punctuation and spelling, and at a steeper price wrote from scratch critiques of books and plays he had only skimmed or, more often, never read at all. No one complained and, holding no degree himself, it amused him to learn that, for the most part, his grades were above average.

It seemed he knew everyone and everyone knew him, but he was treated with only bemused tolerance, or as a convenience. He was obviously a little unbalanced and perhaps completely insane. At best he was an eccentric artist down on his luck, at worst he would eventually bring the authorities into the quarter with their questions and threats and all the rest.

In the meantime, just as they tolerated the deranged boy who stole beer from the back of delivery trucks, or the shaved-headed girl who rode the municipal bus all day from one end of the city to the other, or the naked fool who begged and babbled in the dust near the Cinema Mefou, they saw him as little more than a curiosity which would one day disappear just as mysteriously as it had arrived.

That he might be insane or at least suffering from some sort of emotional or psychological short circuit, he was prepared to accept. If so, it was an illness of long standing. He had always felt like a piece of jigsaw puzzle mistakenly tossed in the wrong box.

That first night, watching her shoot dice and, a few hours later, lying with her damp naked body pressed to his, he had found Bouquet to be the incarnation of whatever it was he was looking for. So, when he stopped returning from his safaris into the quarter, it was to her he drifted. She seemed more prepared than most to accept this strange phenomenon and the days, at least those days before Michel was killed, were good days. The nights were a blur of drink and music and erotic pleasures.

He fell in love with her. Or at least he came close to loving her. He loved as much as it is possible to love when none is returned. He always came close to love. In another way, in another world, he had loved his wife, or had at least once again come close. But Bouquet kept him at arm's length, telling him bluntly that she could not love him. She must protect herself she said.

"You have a wife, Durelle. We are good together, as far as it goes, but you have a wife."

"She doesn't like me. She thinks I'm crazy, she can't even stand having me around."

Bouquet was un-braiding her hair and worked in silence for a moment. "But she loves you," she said at last, "and more important you love her."

What could he say? As best he could, he loved them both. Two women in two utterly separate worlds, their existence touching each other only through him. But what she said was true enough and she was adamant. She could not, or would not, return his love. Offering love to Bouquet was like looking into Bridgitte's cracked mirror, the reflection was twisted and distorted and, sometimes, even ugly.

All they shared was an unexpressed but mutual fear of a darkness deep inside. In the bars and in bed they were allies keeping that darkness at bay in themselves and in each other. Unlike Durelle, Bouquet seemed content to float from day to day on a fragile raft of friendship and affection... until Michel's death set her hidden bitterness boiling like contained lava. Then, striking out, she began to challenge his own pointless drift.

"Why have you come here?"

Listless, he shrugged. "I happened to be in the neighbourhood... looking for something I guess... and I lost my way back."

"Do you think it helped your writing?" She was mocking him, prodding where it was likely to hurt most.

"Everything helps my writing," he grinned.

"Nothing helps your writing," she goaded. "You make no money from it. Did you really imagine going into the streets would help? Who would want to read about... who would buy a story about... this!?" She swept her arm in a wide condemning arc.

He was lying on the sofa, his head resting uncomfortably on the hard wooden arm. He did not open his eyes. "I don't think you understand. What I write no longer matters, only the writing itself is important. The process. It helps me focus, it lets me tame the evil spirits. I do it to understand and define what I see and feel... it's a formula with which to calculate conclusions."

"And what, after all this time and all that writing, have you concluded?" she laughed.

He sighed, "Hemingway had his bullring... Bukowski had his cheap rooms beside the El... I chose the quarter."

He was evading the question, but she would not let him. "I don't know who Bukowski is, but you're not Hemingway... he

made money. How much have you made? What have you concluded?"

He sighed again, "Not a goddamn thing."

It had seemed that death at least, being so final, should have
some definable importance. A death such as Michel's, leaving
such a festering infection among the living, surely had significance.
He had explored it, but everything remained elusive. All the little
boy's death had done was to bring René to life, to make him real.

Michel was gone, but whatever he may have represented to
Bouquet lived on . . . and Melissa was still there.

* * *

At fifteen, Bouquet told him, she had been half seduced and half
raped by an uncle, her mother's senior brother.

The experience had been painful, physically and spiritually, and
while her age mates grew more and more fascinated by boyfriends
and teasing masculine hands beneath their wrappers, she avoided
all further contact with males until the season she turned nineteen.
Then, one night, while serving drinks at a death celebration, she
found herself drawn to a young man from a nearby village.

Unlike the boisterous and rowdy boys she had grown up with,
this young man was quiet and calm and had a smile warm as a
morning fire. It took time, many months in fact, but in the end she
succumbed to his gentle charm. He was leaving for school in the
capital and the night of his departure, she shared his bed.

She told the story with the photo album on her knees, flipping
through page after page of photos of Michel. "One night!" she
laughed in a grim sort of way. "One night was all it took. I was
pregnant." She lapsed into silence staring at the frozen postures of
her dead son mounted on the pages before her.

Durelle already knew that pregnancy had miscarried, so he
asked, "And the boy, the father?"

She cleared her throat. "He never came back from the capital. I
have heard he now lives in Gabon. I've never seen him since our
one night." She laughed again.

"A hard man," Durelle sympathized.

"He really can't be blamed," she shrugged, turning another

page. "He had won a chance to attend university and . . . the way it ended, there was no reason for him to come back."

Three months into her pregnancy Bouquet had left school. She returned to her family and, after the loss of the baby, once again began accompanying her mother to the macabo fields as she had done as a child. But in the following dry season a bridge was begun across the Nyong and she soon followed those girls who abandoned their mother's farms for the bars and dance halls of a town now populated by a hundred free-spending white men.

A few months making her way in the bars, she said, taught her "the lessons of a lifetime," and when the opportunity presented itself she moved in with a Frenchman . . . René.

The rains came and went and by the time the dry season returned again she gave birth to Michel. Less than a year later René's company transferred him to a project in Lourenco Marques. A few short weeks after that, Melissa was born.

"I may be the most fertile woman alive," she laughed again, " . . . and, in those days, I was even stupider than Juliette."

"He knew you were carrying his second child?"

"How could he not know? I was nearly eight months gone when he went away. I looked like I'd swallowed a football!"

"But he went?"

"He was sent away."

Keeping his voice flat, Durelle asked, "But surely he could have made arrangements with his employer . . . to wait for the baby to come, or to have you join him, or even to take you with him?"

"No doubt," she admitted. "But it was not only his company which sent him away. I sent him away."

Durelle said nothing, wondering if that was true, or if it was the whole truth, and if it was, why? But he had not the courage to ask.

After another silence and another page she said. "He left me some money."

Durelle contemplated the refrigerator and the teflon frying pan. "And two children," he said.

"Only one now." She choked and started to cry again and, though he tried, he could not comfort her, she would not let him. She sat, her back stiff, staring straight ahead as tears ran down her face, resisting his attempts to pull her to him, to hold her.

It was in a moment of pause and silence as, through tears, she studied the photo album that Durelle first heard the voice. He heard it clearly and distinctly, though it spoke softly and seemed to come from a distance. The voice said, "I love Bouquet. I have always, and I will always, love Bouquet."

There was no reason that he should have known, but Durelle knew it was René who spoke. He knew it was René before she turned the page and he saw, for the first time, the photo of Michel and Melissa's father. A colour polaroid of a ruggedly handsome man smiling with self assurance as he leaned on the fender of a BMW sports coupe. She did not tell him who the man in the photo was, but there was no need, and betraying little interest in the photo herself she soon turned the page to more pictures of Michel.

Later, many many times, he would try telling himself the voice was a creation of his own jealousy and that it had been born in his own troubled mind or tortured heart when he had seen the snapshot, but even as he tried to believe this, he knew it was not true. He had heard the voice first, "I have always, and I will always, love Bouquet." . . . Then and only then had she turned the page.

Unable to offer Bouquet even comfort, Durelle watched the little girl tearing up an old magazine on the coffee table in front of them. "Melissa is a beautiful child. When she grows up she'll be a real heart breaker. It's the eyes, perhaps. She looks so very much like you." Bouquet cried in jerking sobs. Melissa represented no more comfort than did he.

Melissa was one more part of the dilemma. He could never get a grip upon Bouquet's feelings toward her daughter. She cared for her kindly and gently, but always at a distance. It was as though Michel, the first born and the son, obstinately stood between mother and daughter, leaving Melissa forever at a distance. Michel stood between them in life and in death.

Durelle never once saw Bouquet lay a hand upon Melissa in anger, nor, for that matter, in affection. He never heard Bouquet speak to the child harshly, nor did he ever hear words of love and compassion. His heart went out to the little girl as she would sit quietly in a chair, eyes following her mother's every move about the room. Childish confusion never left those eyes. Durelle came to understand only that he and Melissa shared the same puzzlement about Bouquet. How a woman of such gentle beauty and grace, who must have been aware of how all their lives were anchored to hers, could be so consistently cool and aloof.

Like Melissa, Durelle too watched Bouquet, following her about the most mundane tasks, as if a clue could be gleaned from the way she lifted a cup or brushed her hair. She made him forever expectant. Watching her, it seemed at any moment deeply guarded emotions, hidden away for mysterious reasons, would finally flow out, engulfing them all. It never happened.

Bouquet, to Melissa, was always "Bouquet," never "Mama." Worse still, and with no prompting on anyone's part that he was aware of, she began calling him "Papa." As he had come to hate René, he detested the idea of acting as his stand-in. He was not her Papa and he did not want Melissa to think so.

As Bouquet became more and more distant, withdrawing and wrapping herself in her grief for Michel, he knew his place in their lives, tenuous to begin with, was disappearing. When the end came, there would be pain and he saw no reason why Melissa should share it. Pronouncing "Durelle" was beyond her so he encouraged her to call him Uncle, but she insisted upon "Papa."

Buying the teddy bear was not part of a clearly conceived plan, in fact it had seemed, in the beginning, little more than a drunken whim, but the idea was rooted in more than chance. Bouquet saw to it Melissa was well fed and well clothed and took her directly to the clinic at the first sign of illness, but the child had not a single toy.

Playing with bottle caps had its place, but to Durelle, a little girl should have a doll and the second-hand teddy bear was the closest facsimile he could find in the local market. Also, in some obscure way, he thought perhaps Melissa might be happier if she had a doll or a bear into which she could pour those childish affections which troubled him and bounced off her mother like rain drops striking their tin roof.

Finally, having purchased the bear, he persuaded Bouquet that she should give it to her daughter. He did not want to encourage Melissa's attachment to him by being the one to offer the gift and, as he was certain that somewhere in her heart Bouquet must love the little girl, he had hoped such a gift, coming from her, would do something to remove the searching, questioning look from Melissa's eyes.

Like so much else, the whole undertaking went terribly wrong.

Bouquet offered the newspaper-wrapped package to Melissa and knelt to help her untie the string. Her face shining with antici-pation, the little girl tore away the paper, looked inside and in the next instant went berserk. Consumed by terror she shot across the room and curled in a corner behind the dining table screeching in panic, "Ju-ju Papa! Ju-ju, Ju-ju!"

No amount of effort on the part of either himself or Bouquet could convince Melissa the bear was a "baby" and that she should play "mama." So long as the bear was in sight she cowered be-neath the table and howled in terror, "Ju-ju Papa! Ju-ju!"

Even long after the bear was banished to a footlocker beneath Juliette's bed, Durelle could see the puzzlement with which Me-lissa watched her mother was now mixed with something new . . . distrust and perhaps even fear. Instead of contributing in even the smallest way to binding the wounds of Michel's death, to bringing mother and daughter closer, he had only wedged the knife deeper than ever.

When it was at last obvious his effort had failed he tried to set it to rights. "I guess I fucked up, didn't I?"

"Yes, Durelle, you fucked up."

"I was just trying to . . . " he began to explain.

"I know what you were trying Durelle. But stop trying. I think it's time you stopped trying."

He thought about that for a moment. "But I can't. I don't want to stop trying, Bouquet. I love you."

Still, in the end, he took her advice and stopped trying. He turned his attention instead to René, who he had concluded was the author of all his defeats.

* * *

His fever was high again. The room seemed to contract and shrink and close in upon him. He took another sip of Holy Joseph but that only made it worse. Though he managed to keep it down, it set off another spasm of painful retching. Then, without warning, the little patch of sunlight on the floor opened like a door, and he fell into the shaft.

Consciousness slipped away. He was riding an express elevator. Weightless, sinking down. The light failed, but the elevator continued to plummet. Then it slowed and fell more gently until the plunge into darkness ended and, though it was still dark, it was the darkness of night.

It was raining and he was in a street where the headlamps of passing traffic reflected in puddles formed along the gutters and in pot holes. The light from a few houses and shops shone back from wet pavement, but most of the buildings around him were shrouded in grey and black. He could not see them, but he felt them, hanging above him.

He recognized the place. He was standing at the foot of the path which led to Bouquet's house, though he was facing away, watching a bush taxi parked by the far curb, loading for its journey.

He was puzzled by how it could be there, setting off once more. He had last seen it, smashed against the wall of the beauty salon, the wetness of Michel's blood on its grill sparkling in the brilliance of the afternoon sun. It had seemed beyond repair.

She must have come down from the quarter. Just as on the first night he had not seen her arrive, he simply became aware of her standing beside him. She was saying something he could not hear, or possibly speaking a language he did not understand. She was asking something and he did not know how to respond.

She slipped her hand into his and led him across the street to the little battered bus with its peeling stickers promoting Tuborg Beer and Mobil Oil and Bastos Cigarettes. For the first time he noticed he was carrying his duffle bag. He looked and saw that Bouquet too carried a bag, one that shouted "33 Export" in red and black.

The taxi was full. A dozen blank faces stared through him from rain streaked windows, but the driver and Bouquet were laughing. She led him up a narrow ladder of welded pipe to the roof and the taxi-man threw their bags after them. They curled there, among the luggage and regimes of plantain and sacks of cocoyams, as the taxi swung in a broad U-turn and lurched away.

They lay on their backs and watched the moon dart and dodge through rain clouds, frosting their edges with pale light. In a few places stars appeared like tiny holes in the black velvet curtain of the tropical sky. It was still raining but he had no sense of being wet or cold, though her hand, resting lightly on this thigh, felt warm.

They were moving south. There were too few stars to confirm it, but he knew they were going south. The road was leading them into the rain forest. Soon they were passing through tunnels of giant trees arched across the roadway, their branches, black against even the darkness of the sky, all but blocking out the flashes of moonlight.

Bouquet spoke to him often and sometimes at length, but he could not make out what she said and he did not attempt to answer. His lack of response was of no concern to either of them.

When the taxi emerged from the forest the rain had stopped and they were beside a great river which flowed between low banks and was spanned by a long narrow bridge of steel. The moonlight was bright and clear. They climbed down and stood at the roadside, on the river bank, and watched the taxi roll away, across the bridge and back into the forest beyond.

Once again she led and he followed, down the bank, through head-high razor grass which gripped and pulled at his clothing, to the edge of the water. There, pulled up on the mud bank, lay a long deep canoe, hewn from a single log.

He sat on a rough crosspiece nailed to the gunwales near the bow. She sat behind and pushed away from the shore. He wanted to ask why there were no paddles, but words would not come and she was speaking again in some strange patois and did not seem at all concerned by their uncontrolled drifting on the current.

The river was wide here and seemed very deep. It was the Nyong. He had recognized the bridge, or at least thought he had. It was the bridge built in those seasons when Michel and Melissa were born.

Dawn began to lighten the sky as they floated through a long bend and the river narrowed. The sun rose ahead of them momentarily touching the surface of the water with fire but they were slipping into a strange and silent world of grey.

The current pulled them closer to shore and he saw the banks
lined with trees of the big forest, but all stood tall and straight and
still and naked. There was not a leaf nor a blade of grass nor any
colour save the grey of ash.

The canoe drifted slower, past villages of grey houses populated
by hairless people who were as grey as their huts and the trees and
the crops they cultivated. He watched this living but lifeless world
float by and that world stared back in empty silence.

Ahead, along the bank and standing waist deep in the shallows,
he saw fishermen, grey and bald, casting grey nets into the grey
water in search of grey fish.

The canoe must have touched a mud bar. It stopped near the
fishermen and just below a bank upon which women, naked and
hairless and grey, in groups of three and four, stood pounding
manioc. Their grey pestles fell against grey mortars without a
sound and the fishing nets were cast and struck the water in complete silence.

Bouquet's voice cut the silence calling his name and he turned.
Now, like everyone in this strange colourless river world, she was
naked, but she alone was not grey. Jet-black hair in long braided
tresses fell across her shoulders and round upturned breasts. The
deep copper glow of her skin gave off a light of its own against the
emptiness of the grey colourless existence in which they floated.

She was kneeling on the canoe bottom. She was smiling with her
eyes and with her mouth and she reached toward him, arms open,
beckoning and inviting. The black nest of her womanhood was already damp and glistened in the morning light. He went to her
and she slipped beneath him, moulding herself to him and the
curves of the canoe, raising and opening her knees. She reached
up, her hands soft and warm against his skin. She touched his face
and then slowly let her hands float down across his shoulders and
chest. She spoke to him, her voice deep and husky, the meaning at
this moment clear, though the words were still in a patois he did
not know. As her hands snaked downward one slipped behind, the
fingers sinking gently but firmly into the flesh of his hip, the other
crept forward, grasping and caressing his hardness. She raised her
hips and pulled him toward her and into herself.

Full of hot wetness she held him, one hand behind and one hand in front, pushing and pulling him into her at the rhythm of her own pleasure. He could hear himself speaking in gasps and in the words of a language he only partly understood. The musky scent of her body filled his nostrils and crept in snaking wisps through his head. She lay beneath him, face rolled a little to one side, eyes closed, lips curled just enough to reveal clenched teeth, issuing tiny hissing sounds . . . mind and body, spirit and soul, her whole existence concentrated upon that point where their bodies met.

A shadow passed over the sun, stealing the luminance of her sweat-damp breasts and belly. Her eyes opened and, unfocused, looked past him. He raised his own face a little, and saw René surrounded by the fishermen and pounding women standing waist deep in the current, silently watching. Still, Bouquet pulled him into her and pushed her pelvis against his. Her rhythm increasing just a little as she muttered beneath her breath. Grasping the edge of the canoe with one hand he reached the other beneath her hip and pulled her higher, sinking himself deeper within her.

Suddenly they were wrapped in a net, and then another. Bouquet gasped as he faltered. She clawed at him, pulling him to herself, squirming to keep his sex within her. He looked up again, but too late to avoid the blow as René swung a pounding stick, striking him hard across the shoulders. He lost his grip on the canoe and fell heavily on top of her. She gasped again and groaned a little, then locked her legs about his hips and thrust hard, her nails digging deep into the flesh of his back and his thigh.

Another blow and then another fell across his back. He tried to escape but she would not be denied. She held him to herself like a vice, arching her back and pushing her pelvis against him, holding him within her.

Another fish net was twisted about his face and a pounding stick struck him across the temple. Bouquet rotated her hips and let out a tiny scream in her final ecstasy. She released his thigh and grabbed at his hair, pulling his bloodied face to hers just as a crushing blow fell upon the back of his skull. He heard René's laugh, and the canoe turned over . . .

Durelle's head came up with a snap and cracked painfully against the wall. He was sweating heavily and was nauseous again. He looked at the erection bulging in his blood-caked jeans and groaned.

The air was still, and hot, and sticky. Little rivulets of sweat snaked in trickling tickling lines down his ribs and itched where his belt pinched at his waist. It had been like this, muggy and soupy and difficult to breath, yesterday when he had heard the voice for the second time. At least he thought it must have been yesterday.

The light was going and the room was turning grey.

* * *

The knock had woken him from a dopey, cotton-wool sleep. There was a second knock, but just as he was massing the will to pull himself from bed he heard Bouquet moving about in the outer room. The door scraped across the concrete floor and the voice said, "I'm sorry. I came as soon as I could."

When Bouquet spoke it was in a near whisper and Durelle wondered if it were an attempt to hide the visitor from him or simply because she did not wish to disturb his sleep. "The family has buried its dead."

Taking his cue from her tone, or from some unspoken signal, the visitor lowered his voice as well. They talked for a moment, still at the door, but Durelle could make out nothing more of what was said. When, after some time, they sat in the salon he caught pieces of the murmured conversation . . . though it was more a monologue than a conversation, with René speaking and Bouquet saying little or nothing.

" . . . no one blames you. I do not blame you . . . an accident. . . . We have both lost a son."

René spoke kindly and Durelle thought he heard in that voice hints of a confusion very much like his own. He could not see them, but he knew Bouquet would be sitting, staring into space, perhaps crying a little, but offering nothing. He could picture in his mind that look on her face which said she was polishing the pain inside, greedily keeping it as a bright burning souvenir all her own, one to be shared with no one. René was trying to touch the untouchable.

For a moment, lying in the humid near darkness behind closed shutters and a curtained door, Durelle felt himself drawn, just a little, toward René. As he tried to share in Bouquet's grief, as he tried to comfort her, Durelle could hear René slogging through that muddy killing ground of the spirit he himself had been struggling to cross for so very long.

"...why must you carry this tragedy alone?...pain can be shared...fate has robbed both of us..."

It all sounded very lame at a distance. Silly and trite. Even as the lump of pity and sorrow for the tragic, beautiful woman in the next room rose in his throat, Durelle could not help a wistful smile. René was reciting dialogue he himself had written and rehearsed with Bouquet countless times before. And René came no closer to cracking the armour hard scales of her self-pity.

"...think of Melissa..." René was saying, "why should an innocent little girl suffer so?"

Listening, Durelle closed his eyes and sighed. His conviction that the obstacle to his own futile attempts at reaching Bouquet sat in the very next room, began, in tiny drops, to ebb away. In those few minutes René, his nemesis, might have even been replaced by René a fellow sufferer...had his visit ended at that moment.

But the course and pace and tone of the voice behind the curtain changed and Durelle opened his eyes again. He watched a spider run its web from the light bulb to the ju-ju charm and listened as the words fanned the embers of his resentment and fear.

"...time for a new beginning...far away from painful memories...a new apartment in Paris..."

Durelle held his breath, straining to catch the words, listening for her response. Did she speak though he could not hear her? Was she silently nodding agreement?

"...a good school for Melissa...summer trips to the house in Spain..."

Ashamed of himself even as he did it Durelle sat up and leaned closer to the door curtain, trying to hear her answer. Bouquet made some small sound but if she spoke he could not divine the words. As he had imagined, she was crying again, he could hear only that.

"...I beg you Bouquet...for Melissa, and for yourself, begin again...for me, Bouquet...I love you...I have always, and I will always, love you..."

The words smashed against Durelle with the force of the bus which had killed poor Michel. "I have always, and I will always, love you..." He had heard those words, spoken in the same voice, in the same tone, with the same force, in the moment before Bouquet turned the page of the photo album revealing, for the first time, the photograph of René.

He knew now it had been a warning. Some god or ancestor or spirit had warned him, and he had heard the warning, but he had not understood it then, and he had not prepared himself. Suddenly sweat poured out of him and he looked wildly about the room, searching for something, some response to pending disaster. His panic-stricken search for a way to stop them, to stop René, was arrested by Bouquet's voice drifting, clearly for the first time, through the curtain.

"Go now. You cannot stay here. Go, and let me think. Give me time to think. I will come...tonight...to the hotel."

René protested. He should be allowed to stay a little longer. Bouquet said he should go. He had not seen her for so long and he loved her. Bouquet said that after so many years a few more hours was not forever. He wanted to see his daughter but Bouquet refused to wake Melissa from her nap. In the end, he made her swear she would come to the hotel and Bouquet promised she would be there. The door scraped again and the salon was silent.

Durelle slumped back on the bed and measured the spider's progress. In a moment the curtain was drawn aside and Bouquet stood looking down at him. She had brought a bottle of Holy Joseph and a glass from the kitchen. She half filled the glass and set it by the lantern on the bedside table. The small stand was too cluttered with cosmetics and cassette tapes, overflowing ashtrays and scraps of paper to accommodate the bottle as well so she set it under the chair. Without saying a word she pulled off her kaba and began to dress.

Durelle watched her every fluid move. Watching her dress had for him been one of the pleasures of their life together but all had turned to bitterness. Even the long firm lines of her naked body, the flowing grace of her movements, could bring him no pleasure. He took the glass of country gin and drank. He was plotting the death of René.

Three times as she dressed she refilled his glass and three times he emptied it, and when she was finished at last she left the room and they had spoken not a word.

He heard her rouse Melissa and tell her she must go to stay for a time with her auntie, but Durelle suspected her of play-acting for his benefit, to mislead him.. He could only picture Melissa aboard an aircraft bound for France. Finally, Bouquet and the little girl were gone.

He lay watching the spider, remembering Michel's funeral and how so much more than the body of a little boy seemed to have been covered in that grave.

Drunk, his mind wandering, he recalled another funeral, the death celebration, not of a child, but of an old man of another tribe in the high country to the northwest. He remembered the roaring crash of Dane guns, those home-made muzzleloaders cobbled together from pieces of water pipe and decoratively carved stalks firing black powder salutes to the ancestors. Then he remembered the Banso man who ran a welding shop in the market further up the hill. He had seen a Dane gun fabricated by this smith hanging on the wall of his workshop.

Durelle smiled as the spider spun out a long silvery thread and lowered itself from the ceiling toward his face. He rolled off the bed and stumbled to his feet. He knew how he would kill René.

That a white man might wish to buy a souvenir Dane gun was easily believed. Since the white man knew no better than to pay three times the going rate for black powder and flints, who could resist such a sale? The purchase of a kilo of small nuts and bolts, a hacksaw and a file were everyday sales and prompted no curiosity. In less than an hour Durelle was back in Bouquet's room, sweating and cursing the cheap Nigerian saw blades, as he reduced the Dane gun's long barrel by two thirds.

It was his intention to shorten the gun enough that it might be concealed and smuggled into René's hotel. He had not anticipated the pipe barrel would have been tempered, or that the saw blades would be so soft, but once begun he had no alternative but to complete the job. It took nearly two hours and half the bottle of Holy Joseph before the longer part of the barrel finally fell away. When, at last, it struck the floor, ringing like a bell, he was soaked with sweat. He stripped off his shirt and spent another thirty minutes trying to file down, as best he could, the ragged uneven end of the pipe.

The heat and the gin and the resistance of the Dane gun's barrel fueled his rage, his desire once and for all to remove René from their lives. With René gone he would be able to write. With René gone Bouquet would escape the bonds of her sadness and love him. With the elimination of René, Bouquet would be freed and, once free, would liberate them all. Melissa would have a mother and Michel would come home from school and Fouda could get as drunk as he wished and Bridgitte would be as beautiful as her sister and Juliette would find a white man and . . .

Durelle's hands were bleeding from the effort of cutting and filing the barrel. The muzzle was still ragged and burred but, at last, he had to give up. His hands could no longer hold the tools.

He had no idea how much powder might be required, but supposed half filling the remaining meter of pipe would be enough. He intended to fire at close range. He had forgotten to buy wadding so he tore up one of Bouquet's sanitary napkins and packed it against the charge using a piece of broken curtain rail for a ramrod. Finally he took his three kilos of hardware and, one by one, removed the nuts from the bolts, dropping each one down the barrel of the gun as it leaned against the wall beside him. When the barrel was full to within about five centimeters of the muzzle he took more of Bouquet's cotton and packed it closed, tamping it as firmly as he could.

Exhausted he poured himself another half glass of Holy Joseph and slouched against the wall. He closed his eyes and dreamed of the new and better world he was about to create for all of them. A world over which René no longer cast his shadow, turning Bouquet's radiance from those who truly loved her. Tired and disoriented and drunk, he slept.

He awoke with a start, listening. The room light was on and the web glistened though the spider was gone. He looked up at the window and found only darkness. He knew by the sounds of the quartier that it was already very late, well past midnight. Then he heard the knock.

Someone was at the door and it was the knocking which had awakened him. There was another knock and the door opened. René's voice was calling Bouquet.

He listened for other sounds in the house but heard none. He took mental roll call. Bouquet had taken Melissa with her, to her aunt's she had said, though he still did not believe her. Bridgitte was in the village visiting family. At this hour Juliette would be in a nightclub somewhere. That left only Fouda unaccounted for and he was no doubt in the off-license by the main road. He was alone.

Durelle heard the footsteps in the salon. Slowly he stood up. Silently he closed the shutter against prying eyes and lifted the Dane gun. With trembling hands he fitted a flint and drew the hammer. Still softly calling for Bouquet, René approached the bedroom door. Durelle held his amputated weapon at waist height and levelled it on the curtain. At this range there would be little need for careful aim. There was no light in the salon and as René pulled aside the curtain he squinted into the glare of the bare bulb. He was a full step inside the room before he saw Durelle.

René stopped, too surprised for the moment to speak. Durelle raised his gun a little, pointing it in the general direction of his adversary's chest.

René looked at the blunderbuss and swallowed. "Who are you?"

Durelle found he had difficulty speaking. "You might better ask who I was," he croaked.

René licked his lips and stood very still. "Please put that down. I'm not a thief . . . "

"Yes, you are," Durelle rasped. "You've come to steal the light."

"No, I'm not a thief, I am . . . a . . . I am a family friend. Where is Bouquet?"

Durelle swayed a little, first to one side and then the other. "You tell me, you son of a bitch . . . " He squeezed the trigger and the room disappeared in a blinding roaring flash as the Dane gun exploded. The huge powder charge and heavy wadding hurled a tight pattern of steel nuts through René's chest and the curtain behind him, slamming his body against the door frame. At the same instant, the explosion tore away the poorly welded breach sending slashing pieces of broken pipe into Durelle's torso. Stray bits of the shattered weapon whined through the room raking the walls and smashing the light bulb.

As some semblance of awareness slowly returned, Durelle was amazed to find himself still standing. His ears rang from the crash of the explosion, his nose itched with the smell of cordite and, though the room was in complete darkness, spots of light danced insanely before his eyes.

Even before the pain came to tell him so, he knew he was hurt, hurt badly. His feet were spread wide and planted hard, but his body rocked from side to side and he could not bring it under control. Then the fiery pain began to burn in his belly. He staggered forward, stumbling over what remained of the Dane gun and fell onto the bed.

* * *

The day was fading now. The patch of sunlight had crept across the floor, illuminating for a moment the shattered gun, and begun climbing the wall. It became narrower and narrower and, at last, the yellow band of sun was gone and the room was grey.

Durelle's body shook with fever and his ghosts and visions stalked him.

Fouda was there, drunk at last, staggering back and forth, but still stumbling frantic from task to task, lace-edged panties in one hand, a pressing iron in the other.

Michel spilled blood from the torn pockets of his school uniform into ugly puddles on the floor. In a high-pitched childish voice he obscenely cursed the impotence of both St. Christopher and the Pope and called pitifully for his mother.

Bridgitte sat at the foot of the bed, spitting machine-gun patois as she engaged Juliette in conversation through a piece of broken mirror.

Melissa streaked in terror from corner to corner, howling "Ju-ju Papa, Ju-ju!"—pursued by the teddy bear which had somehow grown the legs of a spider.

From beneath the writing table, where his manuscripts curled and turned to ash, an old man crawled on his belly like a snake. He approached, his decomposing hands holding out the concrete gravestone upon which he offered a drink. Whiskey and coke as always but instead of ice cubes, dice floated in the glass and the number spots were 500-franc coins magically suspended in ivory.

The noise and confusion were unbearable. Durelle closed his eyes and let his head sag against his chest. Then, in an instant, the room fell silent and still, and in the quiet he heard the rattle of curtain rings.

With the last of his strength he raised his face and opened his eyes. They were all there still, Fouda and Michel and Bridgitte and Melissa and Juliette, the crazed teddy bear and all the others. They were staring toward the door where Bouquet stood, her hand holding back the burned and torn curtain. Even the blood-red horseman sat motionless in his clotted saddle, his mount pawing silently at the vomit-stained bed cover.

"Durelle?" She betrayed no shock or fear. Her voice was soft and seemed to come from a great distance. "Durelle, what is it? What have you done?"

He opened his mouth but could not speak. A small trickle of bloody spittle dribbled from the corner of his lips. The sound of her voice was hollow and echoed in his head, but she looked so real.

To Durelle, her casual survey of the room, and the cast which had assembled as though for the final curtain call, seemed a summation of everything he would never fathom and never understand about her. With her look the babble of voices faded and the cacophony of sounds was stilled. Even the scarlet horseman's mount, with one final snort and jingling rattle of its bridle, ceased its restless prancing.

As always her power awed him, but only when she floated through the subsiding confusion was he surprised. Even as she stepped over René's crumpled body she gave it no more than a glance.

For the first time, though only for a fleeting final moment, it seemed clear. The careless, almost crude manner in which she stepped across the remains of her children's father, reaching instead toward him, filled Durelle with a flood of peace and joy such as he had never imagined.

Her words washed over him. A cooling wave, a soft comforting liquid bath carrying away the fever chill and the pain and easing the icy knife from his soul. He closed his eyes as she gently reached out to him.

"Durelle, why? What have you done?"

He spoke but she had to lean very close to hear. "I had to stop him . . . stop him before you and Melissa could go away. When you took Melissa, I knew . . . "

"Oh Durelle, you fool. I have hidden her away with her auntie. He is her father and I am a whore. If he went to the police . . . with money . . . he could have stolen her away."

He grinned a crooked, lopsided smile. "With my money I bought a Dane gun . . . but . . . as always . . . I fucked up." He took as deep a breath as he could manage and rested for a moment. "Have you noticed . . . that everything I do seems to kill from both ends?"

"Durelle, I'm so sorry. The love you look for exists only in your stories. It's a white man's dream. Did I hurt you so much?"

He wanted to answer her, but the words would not come. He wanted to ask her about the Holy Joseph, he wanted to ask if, in preparing her for confirmation, the priest had explained the horsemen of Revelations, he wanted to ask her what she thought love was, but he could not speak. Even had he found some last small reserve of strength, there were no more answers and there were no more questions. All questions were still unanswerable . . . at least in words.

Then she reached out and took his shoulders, carefully lowering him to the floor. Gently she turned him a little and took the wallet from his hip pocket. He could not lift his head to see, and only heard the rustle of the few bills she folded in her hand.

"It was for Michel. Women can always make their way, Durelle, but men are weak." She laughed, bitterly. "Women can always make their way... because men are weak. Like you Durelle."

She stood and went to the door where he could see her again. "I was building for Michel. The rest of us can always find a way. Even Melissa. She will grow to be beautiful and when I can no longer care for her, she will make her way, and will care for me." As she knelt beside René's blasted body and began turning out his pockets Durelle thought she was crying, but he could no longer see clearly and could not be sure. "But Michel... he would have needed more. Like you and René he would have needed much more than life can ever give."

The fleeting tropical twilight disappeared and the light was gone.

About the Author

Ron W. Shaw was born in 1951 on a farm near Perth, Ontario. He studied journalism at Algonquin College of Applied Arts at Ottawa, and has worked on newspapers, radio and television across the province of Ontario.

Since 1974 Shaw has lived almost exclusively in developing countries. He has worked as a photographer on the island of Montserrat, building dikes in Bangladesh, on a cattle ranch in Niger, feeding war refugees in Tchad, with Palestinians in Jordan, digging village wells in Cameroun, as an advisor to the Farm Cooperative Movement in Uganda, and has directed documentary and training films in Tchad, Equatorial Guinea and Cameroun. At present, he travels extensively as a food-aid consultant to Africa, the Middle East, Asia and South America.